MOTHER, WHERE ARE YOU?

A DONNA ROCKFORD MYSTERY

Dorothy Woolfolk

SCHOLASTIC BOOK SERVICES

New York Toronto London Auckland Sydney Tokyo

DONNA ROCKFORD MYSTERIES

Mother, Where Are You?
Who Killed Daddy?
Death of a Dancer
Murder in Washington/Body on the Beach

For Donald, Meg, Mandy, Lisa, Jenny

Cover Photo by Owen Brown

ISBN: 0-590-32519-1

12 11 10 9 8 7 6 5 4 3 2 1   5   2 3 4 5 6 7/8

Printed in the U.S.A.   06

Chapter 1

They were sitting in front of the fire, just the two of them, enjoying a late afternoon snack, when the phone call came.

"Stay there," Janet said. "I'll get it."

She crossed the room quickly and picked up the phone before it could ring again. Her cheerful "Hello!" was followed by a pause, then, "I'm not alone, Mother. Yes, Donna's right here."

Then her breath seemed to suspend in midair, her blue eyes widened, and she cried, "Oh, no!"

She broke into tears, covering her face with one hand, holding the phone away with the other, as if by disassociating herself from the instrument she could ward off the words she had just heard.

In a moment Donna was by her side, reaching for the phone. Janet shook her head. She half-whispered into the mouth-

1

piece, "Mother. When? How did it happen?" Then, "Yes, Mother, I will. I'll start right away." Pause. "Yes. Donna will come home with me." She looked questioningly at Donna, who nodded.

She hung up the phone and said, "My father is dead."

Donna gasped in disbelief.

"I know," Janet said. "We saw him only a few days ago, remember? Saturday."

Janet sat down limply on the sofa. "He was working in his office after lunch, when he collapsed with a heart attack. They rushed him to the hospital, but it was no use." She wiped some tears away with her fist. "The police came and told my mother and took her to where he was." Her voice broke. "Oh, Donna! I'll never see him again!"

Donna, sitting beside her, put her arms around her. She could think of nothing to say to comfort her. She was too stunned herself. Only last weekend they'd seen Mr. Bryson at the football game; then after the game both Donna's father and Janet's had come back to the girls' apartment for coffee and sandwiches. Donna looked about the room, seeing the red linen cafe curtains in the bay window, behind the cushioned window seat; the fire blazing brightly at the other end of the room, beside the comfortable beige sofa she and Janet were sitting on now — the sofa on which Mr. Bryson had been sitting and talking and sipping coffee just three days ago.

And now he was dead.

Warm though the room was, Donna felt a chill run through her. How sudden, and how sad it was. She looked at Janet, whose slender shoulders were shaking as the sobbing girl gave full vent to her feelings. Donna could not see her friend's face; the long brown hair, so like her own, had fallen forward in an unruly mass.

All Donna could do was hold Janet's hand and wait. After a while, the tears stopped, and Janet said, "I told Mother I'd come right home. You heard?"

"Yes," Donna said. "Now you sit there while I pack your things — and mine."

"Thanks," Janet said. "The . . . the funeral's on Sunday. Do you think you can stay down in Washington with me till it's all over?"

Donna said, "Of course I can." She stretched her lithe body, reached up to the top shelf of the closet, and extracted a blue and orange floral weekend case. Her hazel eyes surveyed her friend. "This the one you want?"

3

Janet nodded and said, "What would I do without you, Donna?"

"What would I do without you?" Donna asked. "My parents act like you're their daughter. Which reminds me, I'd better call them and tell them I'm going to Washington with you, and why."

The intercom from the lobby buzzed.

"It's Mr. O'Brien," a voice from downstairs said. "He wants to know if he can come up."

"Yes. No. Not now," Donna said. "Wait. Tell him I'll be right down."

She said to Janet, "It's Pete. I'll run down a moment and . . ."

"He can come up," Janet said.

"It's better if I go down," Donna said. "You know Pete, Janet. He'll want to take over, and protect you, and warn us what to do and how to do it and when to do it."

Janet smiled feebly. Donna patted her on the shoulder and left.

On the main floor she saw him waiting for her — saw his tall, lean-hipped athlete's figure, saw his dark, handsome head and shining black eyes. Big and strong and loving, he waited with an expectant look on his face.

When she told him about Janet's father, he said quietly, "Tell me what to do. Want me to drive you to Washington?"

"Thanks, no." She thought a moment. "What you can do is drive me to my house — if you've got your car."

Five minutes later Pete drove his VW bus into the Rockford driveway and parked behind a small maroon car.

"Take care of yourself." He leaned down and kissed her lightly. "If you need me, call."

"I will. Thanks again, Pete. You're an angel."

She found her mother studying a cookbook in the kitchen, in front of a table loaded with fruits, eggs, flour, nuts. She looked up when Donna came in.

"Donna! I didn't expect you!"

"I didn't expect *you*, Mother."

"Two patients cancelled so I closed the office early. Besides, I wanted to get home for *this*." She indicated her cooking equipment. "What are you doing home, sweetie?"

Her mother was shaken by the news.

"It's a terrible blow for Janet and her mother. I'm really shocked. Of course you can take the car," her mother said.

Donna thought, Mr. Bryson was just about Daddy's age and Mother's, too. Maybe that's why she's this upset.

Mrs. Rockford gave Donna the car keys and said, "Janet needs time. The most wrenching loss of all is when a parent loses a child or a child loses a parent. Be very loving to her."

"Thanks, Mother. For everything."

"Stay there until everything's settled, Donna. And tell her we're here whenever she needs us."

Donna looked at the complicated array of food on the table. Her mother said, "Jamaican fruit cake. There'll be some here waiting for you to take back to school."

By the time she got back to Chestnut Street, Janet was somewhat more in command of herself.

Janet snapped shut the luggage she had packed. "I called Dennis in Fort Lauderdale. I was lucky. I caught him just as he was leaving the boatyard."

"I'm so glad. What did he say?" Donna asked as she began packing.

"He was shocked, of course." Janet's eyes brimmed with tears again. "He said he wished he could come up to be here with me, but it's impossible. His father is on the West Coast on urgent business, and he left Dennis in charge."

"Does he expect you to come down to Florida over Christmas?" Donna asked. The two girls were walking down the steps

6

with the luggage, and Donna was trying to make conversation.

"How can I know what I'll be doing or where I'll be six weeks from now? Everything's changed, Donna. Things will never be the same."

Janet got into the front seat and was silent, her face turned to one side. She stared sadly off into space as Donna drove onto the expressway toward Washington.

Glancing over at her, Donna thought, *She's really suffering. If only I could help her.*

The day of the funeral was dark and cold and rainy. The late October wind whipped through the trees as the family stood around the freshly dug grave. "Earth to earth, ashes to ashes, dust to dust," the minister said solemnly. Janet stood close to her mother, while a pallbearer held a huge black umbrella over their heads.

It was when the coffin was being lowered slowly into the gaping, wet earth that Donna noticed him.

He was standing about fifty feet away from the funeral party — a tall figure in a dark raincoat and brimmed hat, watching the funeral ceremony. It struck Donna as odd. What was the man doing alone, under a tree in the pouring rain? He didn't seem to be part of any funeral party; if he was, where were the others — where was the fresh grave? And why was he watching them so closely?

The ceremony ended, and Janet indicated that Donna was to join her mother and her in the big black limousine. As they prepared to drive off, Donna looked back to see if the lone figure she had seen was still there. He was. He had approached the cemetery plot and was bending over the footstone with its engraved family name, *Bryson.*

"What is it, Donna? What are you looking at?" Janet asked curiously.

"Nothing," Donna whispered. "Nothing at all."

She could not speak of it to either Mrs. Bryson or Janet, say anything to upset them. They had trouble enough without being made anxious over something that was probably nothing.

Inside the Bryson house, neighbors and friends were setting out trays of cakes and cookies and small sandwiches in the dining room. A huge urn of hot coffee stood on the side table. Donna poured herself a china mug of the steaming liquid and warmed her hands against the sides of the mug.

8

On a sofa nearby, a thin, gray-haired woman was urging a piece of layer cake on Mrs. Bryson.

"You'll need to keep your strength up," she said to Janet's mother. "We'll have a long trip down to Florida on Tuesday, you know. I wish you weren't so afraid of planes, Henrietta. The train takes forever."

Janet and Donna exchanged knowing glances. Ever since Janet's Aunt Flora had arrived, she had insisted that Mrs. Bryson absolutely had to come down to live with her in Florida. At first Mrs. Bryson had demurred; but now, forty-eight hours later, they were already discussing the means of transportation.

"That's the way my aunt operates," Janet said affectionately. "Of course she's right. Mother really *should* live with her. The climate will be good for her, they can share expenses, and keep each other company. The moment Aunt Flora started, I knew she'd win the argument."

It developed that Aunt Flora was a great organizer, too. By Tuesday, the moving men had packed up the house; late that afternoon, the girls saw Mrs. Bryson and Aunt Flora off at the train terminal.

Janet and her mother embraced each other tearfully.

9

"Oh, Janet, I hate going so far away from you," Mrs. Bryson said.

"I don't like it either, Mother. But it's the right thing for you to do." She kissed her mother. "We'll be together in six weeks. Christmas vacation. I can earn enough tutoring to add to my babysitting money and pay the fare down."

"You'll do no such thing," said Mrs. Bryson. "You've been through enough. Concentrate on your studies, dear. I'll send you the fare."

That night, Donna and Janet ate dinner alone in the Bryson house, which already looked gloomy and abandoned. The furniture was covered with heavy canvas spreads; cartons packed with dishes, linens, clothing were piled downstairs in the living room, dining room, and kitchen.

They had brought cold cuts, cheese, bread, and soda back with them on their way home from the railroad station. Donna cleared a space on the kitchen table while Janet found some paper cups and napkins and set the table. She seemed abstracted during the meal, eating very little and giving monosyllabic responses to Donna, who had chattered on, thinking Janet was depressed again. But this was more than depression, she realized at last.

"All right, Janet, I give up. You haven't

eaten three mouthfuls and you haven't heard three words I've said. What's on your mind?"

Janet said haltingly, "I didn't want to talk about it, Donna. It seems so heartless ... as if I didn't care ..." She broke off while Donna's eyes held hers. "You know how awful I feel about losing my dad. I loved him so much. And he was wonderful to me. But, Donna, there is one thing ..." She stopped again.

Sudden insight lit Donna's eyes. "Can I guess?" Janet nodded. "Is it about — well, your being adopted?"

"How did you know?" Janet said, incredulous.

Donna reached across the table and touched Janet's hand. "Listen, after living together for almost a year, swapping everything, even wearing each other's bras, and after spilling our insides out to each other whenever something really bugs us — you think I didn't know?"

"Know what?" Janet said fearfully.

"It's the one thing you never talk about, Janet. Once you've told people you're adopted — and you only tell when you have to — you *never* talk about it again." She put a finger to her forehead. "So I asked myself, why does this terrific, beautiful, intelligent creature with whom I live never

11

mention anything as important as that? Not even to me, her best friend?"

Janet squeezed Donna's hand. "You're right. It is about my being adopted." She got up from the table. Her voice was suddenly alive again. "Listen, Donna, at the grave yesterday, I felt terrible — terrible because that was my father going down into it, my father whom I would never see again." Her voice broke. "Still, that wasn't all. What I also felt — I'm ashamed to tell you, I really am, but I have to." She continued in a soft whisper, "Do you know what I felt? A funny little thrill . . . of excitement. There I was at my father's grave and I was thinking, 'Now. Now I can find out!' "

"You mean find out who your real parents are?"

"Yes." Janet took a deep breath. "Isn't that awful?"

"No," Donna said. Her hazel eyes were thoughtful under the clean line of dark eyebrows. "I think I know how you feel. It's only natural to want to know."

"Do you really mean that?" Janet looked at her anxiously. "You *really* believe that it's natural for adopted people to wonder about where they really came from?"

"I think it is. Even when their parents love them as much as your mother and

12

father loved you. That's how the dynamics of behavior work, according to Professor Gordon," Donna said. "Each emotion has its counterpart, its opposite. Like the love-hate relationship between husband and wife, between close friends, even between parent and child."

"I know what you mean. You can both love and hate someone at the same time." Janet let out a deep breath. "Somehow I don't feel so bad now, Donna. You ought to be a psychologist."

"Stick to the subject, Janet. You want to try to track down your real parents, right?"

"Oh, I do!" Janet was serious again. "Every time I asked my father anything about it, he'd stop me. 'You're a Bryson, now,' he'd say, 'that's what really matters. And that's enough for you to know.'" She said unhappily, "But it isn't enough. Can you understand that? I've got to know! Who did I really come from? Who are my real parents? Were they Irish, French, Italian? Were they educated, or plain working people, or what? I don't even know if they're alive!" She started to pace the floor. "This past year, since I met Dennis, it's been on my mind a lot. I don't feel I can ever marry him — or anyone — not knowing who I really am."

"Dennis doesn't care about that," Donna said. "He loves you for yourself. You know that."

"Suppose I've inherited some disease I can pass on to my children someday? I don't even know that."

"It's a possibility," Donna admitted. "But it's very unlikely." Yet as a doctor's daughter, she knew how important it was to know one's family background, medically. If a family had a history of diabetes or heart disease — anything like that — it was important to know and to take precautionary steps.

"I haven't talked about it, not even to you, Donna, because there was nothing I could do about it. I mean with my father not wanting me to stir things up. But now I can start looking."

"Why not?" Donna answered. "I don't see anything wrong in it. Where would you start?"

"My father had a locked file in his den that he never let anyone go near. Well, in the station today, Mother left me her keys — including the one for the file." She said excitedly, "We could go into the den and open that file right this minute!"

"I don't think we should do it tonight," Donna said, seeing Janet's face pale with fatigue. "I don't know about you, Jan, but

14

I'm exhausted. If we get a good night's sleep, we can start on that file first thing in the morning."

"You're right," Janet agreed. She yawned and said, "I haven't slept through a single night since last Friday."

Ten minutes later, lying in a twin bed beside Janet's, Donna waited for sleep to come. Outside, a lonely wind was slamming some bushes against the side of the house, keeping her awake. From the other bed she heard her friend's regular breathing; she had fallen into a deep sleep. Good.

And then there came that odd sound.

Above the howling wind and the bushes rasping and the boards creaking, above all these, there came a rhythmic metallic sound from downstairs. Strange, yet familiar. Then Donna recognized it . . . the sound you made trying to open a lock in the dark. She listened and it came again, and again.

Donna's heart thudded with fear. She couldn't just lie there in the dark and let whomever it was come inside. She rose from the bed and crossed the room quickly. She picked up a bronze student lamp from the desk and ripped the wire from the wall. It would have to do.

Clutching the lamp base in her hand, she went into the hallway and silently down the stairs, feeling her way in the dark. At the foot of the stairs she saw it.

A dark shadow was silhouetted against the wall by the light from outside. She stopped in fear. Someone was outside the door. She held her breath and waited. There was a click . . . was the door going to open? No, something was being withdrawn from the lock. And the shadow moved away.

It took all her courage, but she made herself run to the front door and peer out through the small glass pane near the top.

Through the dark of the surrounding trees, a tall man was running down the walk.

As she watched, he vanished into the blackness.

Chapter 2

Donna woke from a restless sleep at seven o'clock. In the bed beside her, Janet was fast asleep. Taking up her robe and slippers, Donna moved noiselessly to the bathroom, where she washed, brushed her teeth, and combed her hair. Downstairs in the refrigerator she found the few remaining groceries Mrs. Bryson had left behind: some jam, three or four rolls, milk, and cold cereal. As she ate her breakfast she thought back to the night before.

Someone had tried to get into the house. She remembered the man in the raincoat she had seen at the cemetery on Sunday. Was it the same man? If so, what did he want?

Should she tell Janet?

No, Janet had enough problems already; her moods fluctuated enough as it was. It would only send her into panic, probably for no reason at all. The man at the cemetery was probably just a curious stranger. And last night — well, there was lots of crime all over, wasn't there? Just someone trying to break into what looked like an empty house.

They would be leaving Washington for school that afternoon, after the moving men left. There was no point in upsetting Janet, especially when they'd be safely back in Philadelphia that very night.

A half hour later, Janet came downstairs, refreshed and pink-skinned. She ate her breakfast with enjoyment and then pushed her chair back.

"Now?" she said.

"Come on." Donna wrapped the last remnants of food into a sheet of newspaper and dropped it into the trash can. "Let's go."

They hurried to the small room that had been Mr. Bryson's den. Janet was tremendously excited as she fitted the key into the lock on the file cabinet. Donna waited patiently while Janet rummaged through the papers in the first drawer, then the second, then the third. Nothing.

Then Janet pulled open the bottom drawer and shouted, "It's here! I found it!"

With shaking hands, Janet lifted out a

18

manila envelope containing a smaller
white folder with typing on it. It read:

Adoption of Baby Girl,
Aged 10 Months

The two girls stared at each other, wide-
eyed. Together they spread the papers out
on top of a packing box. On a separate
page inside was the name of the institution Janet had come from:

The Perry Home for Children,
Baltimore, Maryland

Other pages gave the name of her adoptive mother and father, the Brysons, their
address in Washington, Mr. Bryson's occupation, financial situation, and refer-
ences. Nothing that Janet didn't already
know.

She looked inquiringly at Donna. "What
good is it? It doesn't have my real name,
the one I was born with. Just the name of
the orphanage I came from."

"At least you have a starting point,"
Donna told her.

"I feel so funny," Janet said, pushing
back a strand of brown hair from her forehead. "Now that I can start to find out
who my real parents are, I'm scared."

Suddenly she was depressed again.

Donna handed her the folder. "Hang on

to this carefully, and let's think about the next step," she said, as they locked the file cabinet and prepared to leave.

That was when Donna remembered having heard her father, a lawyer, tell someone in his office that it wasn't easy for an adopted child to find out who its real parents were. She would have to ask him about that when they got back to Philadelphia.

"I feel bad, Donna. Like I'm doing something I shouldn't." Janet gave a little shudder. "Maybe we should forget the whole thing."

I've never seen her moods change so, Donna thought. Up, down, up, down. She's always been so steady, so calm. This isn't like her at all.

Donna could hardly wait to get back home to speak to her father.

"I don't want to discourage you or Janet," Mr. Rockford said, "but it isn't going to be easy for her to locate her real parents."

It was Thursday morning; Donna had managed to skip a class and invade her father's law office in downtown Philadelphia. Now, as she sat on the edge of her chair, her hazel-green eyes looked at him with disappointment.

"You see, Donna," her father continued, "grown-up adoptees all over America are beginning to look for their real parents. It's part of our new thinking, no doubt." At Donna's questioning look, he added, "I mean, parents and children being able to discuss problems like that openly. Most families are not as free as we are, Donna."

She pushed her long, light-brown hair back and smiled at him widely. "I know, Dad. I sure do."

He smiled back and continued, "What I meant was, there are very few authorities who will open the door to adoption records."

Donna was appalled. "You mean Janet's not going to be able to get the information she needs to find her mother?"

"I mean it won't be easy," her father said gently. "When adoptees start to search for their real parents, in most cases, the only way they can find out anything is to go through birth and death records, look in old phone books, even track down cemetery listings."

"I can't believe it," Donna said. "Why is it so hard?"

"Because children are usually adopted in the first year of their lives. When they start searching at the age of eighteen or older, they have to realize that the real

21

mother and father are probably not living wherever they were years before." Donna nodded, understanding, and her father continued. "People change occupations. And many — most, I believe — adopted children are illegitimate. Finding out the mother's maiden name is difficult enough. But if she has since married someone else, think how difficult it then becomes."

"Oh, Dad, this is going to upset Janet even more."

At that moment, John Harbaugh, Mr. Rockford's young assistant, came to the door.

"Ten-thirty," he said. He smiled at Donna apologetically. "Your dad has an appointment in five minutes with a very important client."

Donna hurriedly kissed her father and left. As she rode the bus up Chestnut Street to the college, she wondered how to tell Janet what her father had said. It's going to depress her even more, she thought.

She still had fifteen minutes until her next class and decided to stop off at the apartment. As she turned the key in the lock, the phone rang. It was her mother.

"What's the matter, dear?" her mother asked. "You sound funny. Not funny haha. The other kind."

"It's Janet, Mother. She's been really down lately, and now I've got some depressing news for her."

She went on to explain, and her mother said, "You've probably both been studying too hard and you're over-reacting. Why don't you bring Janet over for dinner tonight? We're having Cornish hens."

"Oh, Mother. What a great idea! We need a break — we really do."

"Bring Pete too, if you can. He's probably been living on potato chips and peanut butter."

"Mother, I love you. It's just what we all need."

By the time they arrived for dinner, both Donna and Janet were bleary-eyed from studying. Pete had come over to drive them to Donna's home.

As they went up the walk of the big, white, sprawling colonial house, a soft snow was falling. Pete said, "I'm starving."

"That's great," Donna said. "Mother's laying on her Cornish hen dinner tonight. A great rice and mushroom stuffing, and everything that goes with it, including hot apple pie."

"You know, I think that's what I like

most about you, Donna — your mother's cooking."

Donna said nothing. She dropped behind, swooped up a handful of the freshly fallen snow and delicately thrust it down the back of Pete's neck. He howled with surprise and grabbed a handful of snow. Suddenly the front door of the house was thrown open. The three visitors stopped in their tracks. It was not Mrs. Rockford who greeted them. There in the doorway was a vision of sophistication. A feminine slinky figure in a long black sheath, black hair pulled back smoothly and held with an amber comb. Heavy blue-green eye shadow and thick black mascara seemed to weigh the eyelids down over amber eyes. A half dozen gold chains of varying sizes and lengths glittered around the severe neckline, a slit in the long sheath revealed sheer black stockings and black *moiré* Parisian pumps. The total effect was a siren of the early 30's.

Seductively, the siren spoke: "So good of you to come. Really, we're delighted to see you. Donna, my dear . . . Janet . . . and Pe-tah!"

"Has Rudy arrived yet?" Donna said, walking up to the scintillating figure in the doorway.

"Rudy who?" the siren asked.

24

"Why, Valentino, of course," said Donna. She kissed her sixteen-year-old sister on the cheek. "Abbey, you fool," she said affectionately. "What are we made up for this time?"

"I'm simply dressed decently for dinner in our home." She eyed Donna's neat blue slacks and print blouse with distaste. "Unlike you, I don't enjoy roughing it."

"Hi, Abbey," Pete said.

Abbey leaned into Pete's shoulder, threw her head back and through half-closed lids said, "Oh, Pe-tah, I've missed you so."

"Not before dinner," Donna said. "Please. Not on an empty stomach."

Abbey released Pete with an injured look and led them indoors. Dinner was delicious. Even though she was a busy doctor, Donna's mother made a point, especially as the holidays approached, of filling the house with food and love and warmth. And Donna's father, even though a busy lawyer with an equally large practice, not only encouraged his wife, but pitched in and did a fair amount of household duties himself. The only help they needed they got from a cleaning service in town that sent in men — mostly college students — several times a month to do the really heavy work.

When dessert was served, Pete said,

"Mrs. Rockford, the fruitcake is sensational."

"It really is," Janet said.

"How about some whipped cream on it?" Donna's father said, reaching over and dropping a huge spoonful on Pete's plate.

"I'll give you the recipe, Janet," Mrs. Rockford said, "If you want it, that is."

"I'd love it," Janet said.

Donna was pleased to see that Janet was looking lively and relaxed for the first time since the bad news had come. It's my family, Donna thought. Other young people had grave problems with their families. The generation gap was a big one in many cases, and, of course, she'd had her own differences with her parents and probably always would. But what she had that her friends envied was not only their closeness, but their total honesty. The Rockfords could have disagreements, even fights; her father and mother had their own viewpoints on everything from cigarette smoking to coed dorms to marijuana and marriage. But no subject was ever swept under the carpet in her house. You could speak about anything, you could yell, get angry, be hurt and feel it was unfair, but you never felt neglected. Even

26

today, Donna remembered being marched
as a small child through her mother's busy
waiting room full of patients by her Aunt
Carrie, and dissolving in tears on her
mother's lap. No patient was neglected,
but it was important to Dr. Rockford that
her children have close contact with her
even when she was busy.

It was the aura of openness and love
that now seemed so healing to Janet. As
Pete drove the two girls back to school,
Janet said, "Your family is so terrific to
me, Donna. I feel almost together, in one
piece again. I don't know how your mother
does it; she's sensational."

"Right, a regular Wonder Woman,"
Pete said. Then, nudging Janet sitting
beside him, "Like her daughter. Knows
everything."

Donna said, "What I do know is that unless you slow down, you're going to drive
right past our apartment house."

Pete slammed on the brakes. The girls
got out of the car, and Pete said, "Sure
you don't want me to come up with you
two?"

"Pete — go home and study. Please."
Then Donna relented. "I've got my notes
from English Lit. last semester. If you
get stuck, I mean."

"There ain't nothin' wrong with my English," Pete said. "It's poifect." He waved his hand and drove off.

"He's a dream," Janet said. "We're lucky to know two good guys like Dennis and Pete, don't you think?"

"They're lucky to know us," Donna said.

They had started up the stairs and Donna was fumbling for her key when she stopped just outside the door to their apartment.

"That's funny," she said.

"What is?" Then Janet saw it, too. The door, which they had locked before leaving, was slightly ajar.

Donna slowly pushed the door open.

A shocking sight met their eyes. Strewn about the floor was their clothing, books, even groceries from the food cabinet. The apartment was a shambles. Everything had been pulled out of drawers and closets in senseless disarray, as if a miniature tornado had swept through the room and vanished.

Donna felt a terrible sense of outrage. "Who would do such a thing? We haven't got anything worth robbing."

"That's right," Janet agreed. "It doesn't make any sense. Maybe somebody wanted to get even with someone and picked the wrong room."

28

"Maybe," Donna said abstractedly. She continued to make her way through the wreckage, then she stopped and stared at something on top of the bureau. She walked over, picked it up and held it out for Janet to see.

"I think they had the right room," she said. "Look at this."

It was the class photo the girls had been in last year at the end of their freshman semester. The photo was mutilated. Someone had ripped the faces of Janet and Donna out of the picture.

Chapter 3

It made no sense at all.

Later that evening, after they had reported the break-in to the housemother in their building and the police had come and gone, they spent hours putting everything back in order. When they were finished, they sat down and discussed it over a cup of tea.

"What I can't figure out is what they were looking for," Janet said.

"I don't know," Donna confessed. "There's something pretty weird about the whole thing."

"What's that?" Janet asked curiously.

"Actually, it's not one thing, but two. Maybe three."

Janet said impatiently, "Donna, tell me, please."

"It may sound crazy," Donna said, "but maybe someone is trying to — tell us something."

"Tell us something? By ripping the whole apartment to pieces?" Janet said incredulously.

Donna said thoughtfully, "Listen, Janet. Point One, everything was pulled apart, but nothing was taken. Point Two, nothing was destroyed, nothing ruined or ripped, *except* — Point Three, the photograph. Now," she said looking straight at Janet, "why rip the photograph? That's what I can't figure out."

"I don't understand," Janet said, waiting.

"If someone wanted our pictures — for whatever lunatic reason — why not take the whole photo? And there are other pictures of us all over the place."

"That's right," Janet said. Her mood changed abruptly. Donna saw the same sad look come into her wide blue eyes, and a worried frown appear on her face.

Donna said, "What's the matter, Janet?"

Janet yawned and said, "I'm so tired, just all of a sudden. Mind if I turn in?"

"No," Donna said, turning out the light, thinking, she's done that a lot lately . . . escape into sleep. *Why*? She herself lay awake, troubled. Once more she saw the strange man at the cemetery, and the dark figure that had vanished that night at the Bryson home in Washington. Somehow, some way, they *had* to be linked with the ransacking of their apartment. She felt there was very real danger around them. Yet she could think of no possible reason why anyone would want to hurt either of them.

What made it worse was that she couldn't possibly talk to Janet about it, not with the mood she was in lately, so easily upset all the time. If only I could do something to make her feel better, she thought. But what? Maybe Janet would need to see a psychiatrist or a psychologist.

Then she thought of the one person who would know what to do.

Psychology class ended promptly at three. As usual, Dr. Gordon was in a rush. As Donna approached her desk, she was gathering up her books and papers, preparing to hurry to her next class.

"Professor Gordon," Donna said tentatively, "I know you're in a hurry, but can I have a word with you?"

"One word, Donna, that's all," Professor Gordon said, smiling affectionately at Donna, one of her top students. "I have a clinic seminar in fifteen minutes and there's a little pre-thinking I have to do."

"All I want to know is if you can tell me where and how I can get some infor-

mation about adoption. I mean, adopted
people and their feelings."

The teacher looked at Donna's earnest
face, obviously wondering how important
a matter it was. Then she said, "It's a
rather complicated question, Donna, and I
can't answer it just off the cuff." She hesitated. "Why don't you come to my apartment this afternoon? Around five or five-
thirty. Can you make it?"

Donna said, "Oh, yes! Are you sure
you can spare the time, Dr. Gordon?"

"For you, absolutely." She scribbled
something on a sheet of paper and handed
it to Donna. "It's a big old Victorian house
down at 17th and Walnut. I'll be looking
for you after five."

As Donna picked up the paper, Professor Gordon dashed out the door, her
long blond hair swinging, her lean athletic
figure racing down the hall.

Donna was thrilled. She had heard about
the meetings that some students had had
with Professor Gordon in her home. Only
a privileged few ever got to go there, but
their reports were incredibly enthusiastic.
In addition to the fact that the professor
was reputed to make and serve the best
popovers anywhere, everyone who'd ever
been to her house said it was a fantastic
experience just to be with her in such a

personal situation. She couldn't think of any reason why Professor Gordon should have extended the invitation to her.

She could hardly wait till five o'clock.

A clock was chiming in the hall as Professor Gordon let Donna in. The moment she stepped inside, Donna felt that wonderful ambience the senior students talked about. The room was huge — high ceilings and a big bay window overlooking a stretch of garden made it seem even bigger. On one side, a fire had been lit and its soft glow against the gray November dusk was heartening. In front of the fire, on a low table, a copper Russian samovar stood beside a tray with a delicate bone china tea service set out.

Profesor Gordon took Donna's dripping raincoat and said, "Sit here by the fire and warm up a bit. I'll be back in a flash with some popovers." At the gleam in Donna's face, she added, "You've heard?"

Donna said, "I sure have. When I was a freshman last year, the first thing I heard from the upperclassmen was, 'You're no place until Professor Gordon invites you to her house. And you've never eaten anything until you've tasted her popovers.'"

Dr. Gordon whistled. "How can I possibly live up to such advance notices? And I certainly won't if I don't get into the kitchen and save the batch I have in the oven."

A few minutes later she was back with a platter on which there were half a dozen steaming popovers and a crock of fresh dairy butter nestled beside a jar of strawberry preserves.

When Donna tasted the first popover, she said, "It's great. My mother makes them — she's a sensational cook — but they're not as fabulous as these."

"I'll give you the recipe to take to your mother." Professor Gordon poured tea into their cups and said gravely, "Now, Donna, tell me what the problem is."

Donna told her how Janet had been behaving since the death of her father; how moody and upset she was; and how guilty she felt about looking for her real parents.

"Strange you should bring this up now, Donna," Dr. Gordon said. "I'm doing a paper on it. You see, it's only recently — in the past two or three years — that the whole question of adoptees searching for their biological parents has arisen." She took a sip of tea. "More and more adopted children, as they grow up, want to know who their real parents are." She added softly, "Most of the ones searching are women. And, most often, it's when they are about to become mothers themselves."

"Actually, my friend is only nineteen. She isn't married and she's not going to have a baby. She has been going with someone . . . but I don't think that's the real reason." Donna considered a moment. "I think it has something to do with her father — her adopted father. He died about two weeks ago, and now that she feels she might learn about her past, she feels very guilty."

"She shouldn't feel guilty," Professor Gordon said with authority. "An eminent group of psychologists studying adoption has found that there are three major reasons why an adoptee begins a search. The first is when an adopted female is about to become a mother herself; naturally, she begins to wonder about her own background. The second reason is the need for some kind of special information about her health or genetic background. For example, if one of her real parents had an illness that might be inherited or passed on — well, a prospective mother should know. Don't you agree?"

Donna said, "Sure. It's the first thing I would want to know."

"Of course." Dr. Gordon offered the platter of popovers to Donna, who grinned sheepishly and took another one.

"I could very easily become a popover freak," Donna said. "I'm sure they're terribly fattening."

"I'm sure they are," Professor Gordon said. She looked approvingly at Donna's slim, shapely figure in its trim blue jeans and fitted body shirt. "But you don't have to worry. You watch your diet, don't you?" Then, as Donna nodded, "Then splurge this once — have some more strawberry jam and butter — and let's get back to your friend's problem.

"The third and perhaps most traumatic reason adopted children start out to search for their parents is the death of an adoptive parent. All these years your friend has probably been very anxious to know who her real father and mother were, but probably did not want to hurt her adoptive parents. Now that she has the opportunity — since her adoptive father died — she feels guilty about going ahead."

"That's exactly right," Donna said.

"She must not give in to that feeling of guilt. The more information we have about our past, the better able we are to deal with our present, and our future." Dr. Gordon put her teacup down. "Tell your

37

friend, Donna, that her curiosity is the most natural thing in the world. Tell her there's no reason for her to feel guilty."

"Oh, I will. I'm glad I came to you, Dr. Gordon." As the clock struck the hour, Donna rose from the sofa. "I can't tell you how grateful I am." She sighed. "I only wish I didn't have to tell Janet what a hard job lies ahead."

Dr. Gordon studied Donna's face, then said warmly, "Your friend is lucky, Donna. I have the feeling that you'll help her find the answer — somehow. Go to it, my dear."

A half hour later, back at the apartment, Donna repeated Professor Gordon's information.

"You're not making this up? She really said it's okay — the way I feel?" Janet asked anxiously.

"That's right, Jan. She said it's only natural. You're just going to have to drop that anxiety trip you've been on." Then, as her friend's face relaxed into a faint smile, Donna repeated the information her father had given her.

Janet took it very well. "All right, so it won't be easy. But he said it can be done, right?"

"Right."

"When can I start looking — and how do I start?" Janet asked.

"Not 'I,' sweetie. 'We.' I'm in this investigation with you, remember?" As Janet nodded, Donna continued, "I'll be busy with the lab right through the weekend. I think I can take Monday off. How about you?"

"It's okay," Janet said. "I can skip biology class. What do we do?"

"We trek on down to The Perry Home in Baltimore and start asking questions."

Janet jumped up. "Oh, Donna, that sounds great!" She started to laugh happily. "Come on. We're going down to Pagano's and I'm treating. We'll split a pizza."

Donna pulled on her ski jacket. "Not me. I'm dieting. But I'll watch you make a pig of yourself. Let's go."

"I don't think you should go down to Baltimore," Pete said. "I don't like the sound of that break-in at all. Maybe some madman is out to get one of you."

"If someone is out to get us, I'll bet there's a method in his madness," Donna said. "The thing is, what we'll need is a car, Pete. Do you think you could . . .?" Donna looked at him questioningly.

39

"Sure, sure. But I wish I could drive you down there," Pete said worriedly. "You really ought to have a man with you."

"Pete!" Donna said, warning him.

"I know. Who needs a man? A woman is just as good as a man." He laughed raucously.

"Not funny," Donna said.

Janet pushed the handle of the door and began to get out of the car. "If you two are going to start the battle of the sexes again, I'm getting out." She beamed a smile at Pete. "Thanks for driving us home. I've got a mass of biology to learn by tomorrow."

The moment they were alone, Pete said, "You know I'm against Janet's doing one single thing about all this. Who knows what she'll find out? Maybe her mother will turn out to be someone she's ashamed of. Or maybe they'll fall into each other's arms and Janet will have to split her feeling for Mrs. Bryson and her real mother."

"Pete, you just don't understand," Donna began, and then she stopped. What's the use? she thought. Pete's always getting off on some other wavelength from me. It never happens with Janet. Is it Pete — or just men?

"I'm going to miss you, babe," Pete said, pulling Donna close to his chest. Donna could not help responding to his kiss. In his arms, she thought, I wish I didn't feel this way about him. We're not right for each other.

On the way down to Baltimore, Donna decided to hold no more secrets from Janet. She told Janet about the man at the cemetery, and then the stranger at the Bryson house the night Janet's mother and aunt had left for Florida.

Janet was not impressed. "Coincidence. That's all it is. I don't believe anyone is following us, or me. Why would they? We're nobody."

"Janet, I don't know why, but I can't accept 'coincidence.' Something tells me that there really is something we don't understand going on."

Janet said, "You have some imagination."

"I hope it's only my imagination." She handed the road map to Janet. "Can you find Mulberry Street? That's where the hotel clerk said we should turn off."

In the dark of the car, her eyes squinting, Janet said helplessly, "We might as well be in Hong Kong. And this map could be in Chinese. I can't read anything in this light."

Just then Donna yelled, "There it is!

Route Number 6!" She swung the car smoothly onto the exit road. A few minutes later, they checked into the Monmouth Inn. As they waited for the hotel clerk to find their reservations, they looked at their surroundings and what they saw pleased them. The lobby — old and dark and walnut paneled, with deep red leather armchairs, and huge tapestry sofas — had against one wall a huge, authentic, original fireplace of greystone blocks. In it a welcoming fire was ablaze, sending out waves of warmth. Except for the electric lamps here and there, the atmosphere was that of an 1850 inn. They were delighted.

As they came into the lounge, a tall, dark man in a heavy overcoat, wearing a brimmed hat, turned away from the desk and with his head down hurried past them so roughly that his shoulder knocked into Janet's. He did not apologize as he hastily went out the door.

The room clerk told them they had missed the dinner hour, but, "You can get a very nice snack in the Stirrup Room," he said. When he looked at the cards they signed in on, he said, "That's funny, a man was just asking for you."

"He was? How can that be? We don't know anyone in Baltimore," Donna said. "It must be a mistake."

42

"Oh, no," the clerk said. "He asked for you by name — Rockford, Bryson. No doubt about it."

The two of them could not figure out who the man could possibly be. Upstairs, as they unpacked their overnight bags, Janet said, "It's impossible. No one knew we were coming to the inn tonight, except your family and Pete. We almost didn't know it ourselves until we actually called The Perry Home yesterday and made a reservation here." She hesitated. "Maybe he's got us mixed up with someone."

Donna said, very gravely, "I don't like it. The man at the cemetery, the break-in at our apartment, and now a strange man asking if we've arrived in a place where we hardly knew we really would be. It all ties in. It has to. I just don't know which one of us he's interested in."

Janet intercepted her with, "That man — did he look like the one at the cemetery?"

"I'm not sure," Donna said. "I think the man at the cemetery was shorter and heavier. But they both had on dark overcoats . . . and hats, don't forget that."

"What do you mean?"

"A hat is a pretty good way of disguising an identity. It not only shields part of the face, but it conceals the hair, its color and style, the works. A man with a brimmed hat can just drop his head a little, like this one did, and it's hard to recognize him even up close."

Janet said, "That's logical. Maybe you should be a lawyer — or at least someone who has to use logic in his job."

"*Her* job," Donna said. "Where is it written that lawyers and other professionals have to be men? Do you know how many times I answer the phone at home or go to the door and when I say 'Dr. Rockford isn't in,' they say 'Oh, when will he be back?' I mean if it's a stranger or a new patient. And every time I tell them Dr. Rockford is a woman, there's this dead silence."

"You don't have to get so excited," Janet said.

"I'm not excited. It's just that the things I'm most interested in are supposed to be 'man's work.' "

"You mean abnormal psychology? At least one third of your class is female, Donna."

"I know," she agreed, "but what really steams me up is this." She thrust a textbook toward Janet.

Janet read aloud, " 'The Criminal Mind, Its Psychological, Psychophysical, Hereditary and Environmental Aspects.' " Then she said, "So what?"

44

"So look at the authors of the chapters, will you?" She turned several pages and started reciting names: "John Martin, Hans Reichman, William Clarkson . . ." She broke off disgustedly. "Nineteen authors, and not a single woman authority among them. Investigating crime is obviously a male pursuit."

"Why are you so upset?"

"Because, liberal and liberated though my parents are, I think they'll kick up a fuss if I really opt for criminal investigation as a career."

"Why?"

"Because there's a certain amount of danger attached to it, I suppose."

Janet said, "Knowing you, I'm sure you're not going to let that stop you. Right?"

"Right," Donna said, and thought: Finding your real mother is my first case. If I can only handle it well, maybe I can get Mom and Dad to agree it's what I should do after college.

Later that night, in bed, Donna wrestled with the problem of the stranger who asked for them. She thought of several innocent explanations, but none of them satisfied her. Finally, she forced herself to sleep. They had a big day ahead of them tomorrow.

Their first stop would be the institution Janet had come to the Brysons from eighteen years before — The Perry Home for Children.

Chapter 4

The building was a far cry from the gloomy, dark "orphan asylum" the girls had read about in stories like *Oliver Twist*. In the cheerfully decorated office, sunlight streamed across bright orange and blue walls. The blonde woman seated behind the desk was attractive and young.

Seeing a placard with the name "Mrs. E. Fitch," Janet said, "I phoned you yesterday, Mrs. Fitch, from Philadelphia."

The young woman smiled. "I'm just holding down the desk till Mrs. Fitch gets back. My name is Pamela Chapman."

Donna said, "When we phoned yesterday, we were told to speak to Mrs. Fitch about what we needed."

The young woman nodded. "Then you'll have to wait for her. She's the matron. I don't work directly here; I'm a caseworker."

She was very friendly and in a moment

47

the girls were sitting down beside the desk while Janet told her their reason for being there.

Pamela Chapman was instantly sympathetic. "I can understand your wanting to find your real parents, Janet. It's funny, but for years we had very few requests of this type. In the past year or so, however, there are many people — usually your age or older — who come in and want to look at their adoption papers."

Donna and Janet looked at each other, pleased. It was encouraging news. So Janet wasn't a special case.

"Do you mean they'll let us see the records?" Donna asked.

"It's not that easy," Pamela Chapman said. "But there are ways of getting the information."

The door swung open and a large, stern-faced woman entered. She strode to the desk and said with authority, "*I'm* here now, Miss Chapman. I'll take over."

Pamela Chapman rose from the chair and said, indicating Janet, "This is Janet Bryson, Mrs. Fitch. She's here with Miss Rockford about her papers. I was just telling them..."

Mrs. Fitch cut her off. "I said I'll take over." She sat down in the chair as Pamela walked to a file cabinet nearby and opened a drawer.

"If you had mentioned the exact purpose of your visit in your phone call yesterday, Miss Bryson," Mrs. Fitch said to Janet, "I could have spared you the trip."

"I don't understand," Janet said.

"What I'm saying," Mrs. Fitch said carefully, "is that we don't have information of that sort available at a moment's notice. This is a very big institution. You should have given us more time."

At the file cabinet, Pamela Chapman's head was inclined toward them, obviously taking in the conversation.

Mrs. Fitch turned abruptly and said, "Miss Chapman! Couldn't you tend to that later? I'm trying to have a conversation with these young ladies."

Pamela accepted the rebuke gracefully. "Of course, Mrs. Fitch. I'll come back later." She left the room noiselessly.

Mrs. Fitch said, rather more friendly, "What I will do for you, Miss Bryson, since you've made the mistake of coming all the way down here without following proper procedure" — her eyes were expressionless through the lenses of her glasses — "what I will do for you is look into the master file. It covers all of our

49

adoptions for the past twenty-five years. How old are you, anyway?"

Janet said, "I was nineteen last month."

"I'm not sure I'll find anything. Don't get your hopes up." Mrs. Fitch opened the door and left them alone.

"She's like a tough Marine sergeant," Donna said.

"Right. She's frightening."

"I think she puts on that act to keep people in their place. Either that or she's naturally nasty."

"Donna, I have the rottenest feeling here." Janet pointed to her stomach. "That sinking feeling I always get when I think I'm going to fail at something."

"I feel sorry for the kids in this home if they have very much to do with her. She probably makes old Scrooge in *A Christmas Carol* look like an angel of mercy."

They were both laughing when Mrs. Fitch returned.

She said coolly, "I've given them the details in the file room. They should be calling me here very shortly."

Mrs. Fitch returned to her desk and went through a stack of mail as the girls made small talk for a few minutes; then the phone rang. Janet sat tensely on the edge of her chair, waiting, as Mrs. Fitch said, "Yes, yes. Oh, no? I see ... I see."

50

She hung up the phone and said, with a small smile on her lips: "Exactly as I thought. There is no record at all of your adoption." She let that sink in, then added, "Of course, if you knew your original name, it might be a different matter."

Janet said, "But that's why I'm here, Mrs. Fitch. To find out who my real parents are. What their real name is."

Mrs. Fitch leaned forward, raising her eyebrows. "My dear, most of the children who come to this home have only the mother's name on their records. I'm sure you understand why."

Her meaning was inescapable. *Their mothers are unmarried. Undoubtedly yours was, too.*

Janet fell silent. Donna said, "Do you have any suggestions, Mrs. Fitch?"

"I'm afraid not. Without Miss Bryson's original name — the one under which she was brought to this agency — we can go no further. If you ask me, it's just as well. Why go around stirring up trouble?" She shuffled some papers on her desk. "Now, if you'll excuse me..."

It was two disheartened people who left The Perry Home. Going down the steps of the building, Janet said, "I told you. I

51

knew we weren't going to find out anything."

Donna said, "For heaven's sake, Janet, let's not give up hope. We're not stopping here, I can assure you."

As they waited a moment to get their bearings, a woman stepped from a car in front of the building. She was tall and slim and blonde and she was smiling at them. Pamela Chapman.

"Quick," she said. "Get into the car. I want to speak to you and I don't want that old battle-axe to see me."

Donna and Janet got into the back seat and Pamela drove them to a tree-lined street where she parked the car and then spoke seriously to them.

"Look, I don't know if I can help you or not. But I'm certainly going to try. Mrs. Fitch isn't very pleasant ... as I'm afraid you saw. I've seen her use every tactic to keep adoptees like Janet from finding out what they want to know."

Janet said, "I really appreciate this. But I hope you won't get into trouble by trying to help me."

Pamela Chapman shook her head. "I won't. But the less Mrs. Fitch finds out, the better. Of course, I won't do anything illegal. There's very little I can do myself. I have some suggestions for you, that's all.

My first suggestion is that you go to the City Hall here in town. All adoption records are kept there." She added, "I'll go with you, if you like."

"That's very good of you," Janet said. "Won't we be taking you away from your work, Pamela?"

The blonde young woman shook her head. "Actually, I need some information from one of the buildings not too far from City Hall. Come on."

By the time Pamela pulled her car up in front of the City Hall, Janet was feeling so optimistic that Pamela warned, "Don't get your hopes too high, Janet. This is only one step along the way. It's a long chance, really, but worth taking."

They mounted the steep gray steps and went through the massive doors of the City Hall to an ancient elevator that took them to the third floor. There, in a dark-green dingy room crammed with file cabinets of all sizes, a clerk behind the counter greeted them.

When they told him the purpose of their visit, the clerk said, "The laws of this state are very clear in the matter of adoption. The records of adoption may be seen only by someone with a court order." Then he added, "And you have little chance of getting it, I can assure you. The minute a child is adopted, the court records are sealed. It would have to be something a lot more important than plain curiosity for a judge to order the seals broken."

The clerk, with an air of importance, went back to his work. Obviously, they had reached a dead end.

Pamela said, "I'm sorry. Someone in the Welfare Department told me that the state had changed the laws about their records. I would have checked it out before this, but there was no need until today."

"It's all right," Janet said. "I appreciate your trying." She tried to sound more cheerful about it than she felt, but even Pamela was not fooled.

When they got back in the car, Pamela said, "I feel deeply for you, Janet. And for young women like your biological mother. In the past — in your mother's case, nineteen or twenty years ago — young girls like her were often forced by the morals of society to give their babies away. An unmarried mother was usually pressured by her family in no uncertain terms to give the baby up. What a painful thing for a young girl to have to do, unless she wanted to . . . give up her child, and then never be able to see it again."

Janet touched her arm. "Thank you, Pamela. You understand. But people —

54

even Donna — have warned me that if I do find my mother, and perhaps my father, I may be stirring up trouble."

"They may be right. But when an adopted child is fully grown up and has a desire as strong as yours to learn her real background, I feel it is only fair that she have the chance to do it." She made a little grimace. "I'm afraid I haven't been much help, though."

"What you've done is make me know that I'm not giving up," Janet said quietly.

Donna squeezed her hand. "Good girl," she said. "Because if you gave up now, I'd go on by myself. We're both in this to the end."

Pamela looked at her watch and said, "Oh, my, I've got to go. Tell you what, give me your address and I'll see if I can come up with anything." She reached into her purse and pulled out a card. "If you need me you can always reach me either at The Perry Home or at this address. It's where I live."

When she was gone, Janet asked, "Now what?"

"Now we get back to school — fast. I'm worrying about our exams. That okay with you?"

Janet nodded.

Donna said, "You know, one good thing

about having to go back early, we'll be able to see the gym tryouts."

"That's right," Janet said absent-mindedly.

"And I may get a chance to sign up for karate. Pete's determined that I learn it." She was trying to make conversation, but Janet was back in a mood again.

Donna thought, She's worrying about our next move. Well, so am I.

We've got to pick up the threads of the search somehow. But where?

The gym exhibition lasted much longer than they'd expected. It was Pete's room-mate who brought the news to them.

"Pete wants me to tell you that he won't be doing his stuff until almost 11 o'clock. He wants to know if you can wait that long, Donna."

"I don't think so. I've got that psych paper to do." Donna turned to Janet, who said, "I have a paper to do for biology. I haven't looked at a book."

"Tell Pete we're sorry. But I'm glad I don't have to be his karate victim in the demonstration," Donna said.

"You know Pete," his roommate said. "If he wants you to learn karate, he'll never let up until you're an expert. That's what makes him such a great instructor."

"Yes — he's a terrific pest, isn't he?" Donna laughed as they walked out.

Janet drew her coat collar closer as the cold wind whipped the snow now falling heavily about them, stinging their faces. They were quiet as they passed between the huge oak trees that bordered Graduation Walk. It was a lonely part of the campus; at this hour on a winter night, it was more desolate than ever. There was no one in sight.

They did not see the dark figure that stepped out from the shadows behind them. His footsteps made no sound in the thick snow that covered the walk. It was only when Donna saw his shadow reflected in the snow from the dim light of a street-lamp arc that she turned around. By then it was too late. Before she could shout a warning or take a step to help Janet, the attacker struck a mighty blow with some heavy object he held in a gloved hand. He caught Janet off guard with several assaults on her head, face, and neck, as Donna slipped through the snow toward him. As she reached him, she clung to his upraised arm and kept him from striking again. She heard a heavy sigh from Janet, whose eyes were closed in a bloodied face as she dropped to the ground.

Donna could not see the attacker's face — it was completely covered by a ski mask.

She screamed, "Help! Help!" even as she started kicking and banging away at him. She tried to remember something, anything that Pete had shown her in their one karate session, but failed. All she could do was swing wildly and try to kick out at him with her foot. It was completely ineffective.

In one swoop he had her, holding both her wrists in one big, incredibly strong hand, while with the other he raised the weapon to strike her. But in that instant a group of students burst into the path from up ahead. He turned his head and Donna seized the moment to make one final effort to break free. Incredibly, it worked. Her attacker released her so suddenly she fell to the ground as he sped into the darkness.

A student ran up to Donna and, helping her up, asked, "What happened?"

"Never mind me," she said urgently. "Please! Go after him!"

Two of the three ran in the direction Donna was pointing. The third, a young woman, said anxiously to Donna, "What happened?"

Donna said, "Stay here with her, please,

while I get help. And be sure not to move her!"

Donna looked down once more at her friend lying motionlessly in the snow. Under the swath of blood on Janet's face, her skin was ashen white. Her eyes were closed, and her face held the repose of a death mask.

Chapter 5

She ran through the falling snow quickly to the public telephone inside the library. She hoped she would be able to get in. Sometimes the outdoor corridor was locked, sometimes it wasn't.

Tonight she was lucky; the library door was open. She ran to the phone, and with frozen fingers fumbled for a coin and dialed her parents' number. When her mother answered, she said only, "Janet had an accident, Mother. I'm afraid she's badly hurt."

After Donna had explained, Dr. Rockford said, "I'll phone University Hospital to send an ambulance to where you are. Ride the ambulance with her, Donna. I'll meet you both at the hospital when you get there." She paused a moment. "You haven't moved her, have you?"

"Mother, you know I know better than

that — especially when she may have some kind of concussion or fracture."

"Good girl," her mother said. "See you soon. And don't worry. We'll take care of her."

Donna's random diagnosis — a concussion — was what it turned out to be. And, in falling, Janet had injured her ankle.

"Are you sure she'll be all right?" Donna asked her mother anxiously.

They were standing beside Janet's sleeping figure in the bed. The white hospital walls were in shadow now; only a small bed lamp lit the room. In the past half hour, Dr. Rockford had completely checked Janet over. Now she consulted the clipboard on which she had listed her report.

"Concussion, lateral," Donna read over her mother's shoulder. "What does that mean? How bad is it? And what about her ankle?" Donna persisted.

"Donna, please," her mother said. "Come outside and I'll tell you all about it. But first you'll have to talk to the police sergeant outside."

"Police?"

"I had to notify them," Dr. Rockford

61

said. "A case of assault . . . it's the law, dear."

The tall, blue-coated officer was waiting for them in the lounge. "We've done a thorough search of the grounds, Doctor," he said. "But, frankly, there's nothing yet."

After questioning Donna, the police officer finished taking notes, snapped his book shut, and said, "It's worse than looking for a needle in a haystack. In this snowstorm, on a campus this big, and with an attacker whose face was covered with a ski mask that he's taken off by now — we don't stand a chance of locating him. Not a chance."

After he left, Donna sat down beside her mother on the sofa.

"Janet will have to be hospitalized for about a week. Luckily her ankle is not broken — only badly sprained. She'll be up and about wearing an ankle brace within a few days. Her jaw is bruised — it's not easy for her to talk or chew food. I've put her on a liquid diet."

"There really is nothing to worry about? You're telling me the truth, Mother?"

Her mother said, "Yes. Barring complications, she's going to be fine. We have to watch the concussion carefully, of course. But I truly don't anticipate any problems." Her voice sharpened. "Now I want you to tell me the truth. That was a pretty serious assault, you know. Whoever it was probably meant to do much greater harm. Janet's heavy winter clothes saved her."

Donna said quietly, "Mother — you think someone may have wanted to kill Janet?"

"Yes. Or you." Her mother's eyes were piercing, searching Donna's troubled hazel eyes.

It was time to tell everything she knew. Donna said, "Mother, I'm pretty sure I'm not the one he's after."

By now they were walking through the darkened lobby downstairs. "I think you'd better come home with me," Dr. Rockford said. "What this needs is a family discussion. Don't you agree?"

Before Donna could answer, the revolving door swung around and there was Pete, out of breath from running.

"I heard about Janet and came right over." He stopped to take a breath. "How is she?"

Dr. Rockford looked into Pete's dark brown anxious eyes. "Come along with us, Pete. We'll explain on the way."

When they were all together in the living room — Donna, her parents, her sister Abbey, and Pete — Donna told them everything that had happened before tonight.

As she finished, her father said, "I can

63

understand your wanting to help Janet. As you know, I've instructed John Harbaugh in my office to give you any assistance he can. But don't you think this has gone far enough, Donna?"

Donna said slowly, "Dad, how can I stop? Someone is certainly out to harm Janet."

"What makes you think it's just Janet?" her father asked.

"Because," Donna said, "I first saw the strange man at Janet's father's funeral. Two, it was Janet's house someone was hanging around in Washington. Three, the man asking for us was in the Monmouth Inn, which is in Baltimore, not far from The Perry Home — where Janet was placed before she was adopted." She said to her father reasonably, "Don't you see, it all has to do with Janet? If anyone wants to hurt me, he can do it right here in Philadelphia. No, Dad, it's definitely Janet — not me."

"You're convincing me," her father said. "But it doesn't alter anything. With you helping her, you're both in danger. This last was a violent physical attack. Whoever it is, I'll go along with the theory that his motive is somehow involved with the two of you trying to get information about Janet's past."

"Janet has a right to know. You can't expect us to stop now," Donna said.

"Your father is right," Pete said. Donna gave him a warning look, and he added, speaking to Dr. and Mr. Rockford, "Do you suppose if Donna promises to be more careful, and to check out any big moves she plans to make . . . ?" He broke off, but his penetrating brown eyes held their attention.

After a long moment, Donna's mother said, "That would be all right with me, Pete."

Donna's father said, "And with me — *if* she's very careful about where she goes and what she does, and *if* she checks out any major moves in advance with us."

"I like the way you're all speaking about me as if I weren't here," Donna said.

"It's because we're all worried about you and Janet," Pete said, as Abbey suddenly flung an impulsive arm toward him, touching his hand with tentative, purple-tinted fingers. Donna noted that her sister had taken time, despite the emergency, to apply lipstick and mascara and a spray of Tiger Woman.

Abbey said with honeyed admiration, "Pe-tah! You're so wise. Oh, I do admire that man's mind of yours."

"Go to bed, Abbey," Dr. Rockford said.

"Staying up late seems to be unhinging your brain. 'Man's mind,'" Donna said. "Where'd you dig that up?"

Abbey rose with a wounded expression and went upstairs, wafting her pale lemon chiffon negligee behind her.

Mr. Rockford said with amusement, "Don't be too hard on her, Donna. This is just a phase; she'll grow up, I'm sure."

"I can hardly wait," Donna said. "She's setting back the Women's Movement ten years, acting so helpless and idiotic."

"When you were her age, you were always playing detective — acting the part of the Great Psychologist," her mother said. "Every move your father and Abbey and I made was dissected by you. 'What do you mean by that?' was your favorite expression. It drove us wild."

"I remember," Donna said. "I guess I was pretty terrible."

"Never," her father said. "But you were — and are — very strong-minded. What are we going to do about you and Janet?"

So they were once again back into the problem. They talked for another hour; by the time Donna said good night, there was agreement all around. *Proceed with caution* was the guideline.

"We're relying on your good common

sense," her mother said, as Donna got into the car for the drive home.

"Don't worry," Donna said. "I'll be super careful from now on. And I'll check it all out with you and Dad."

"And me," Pete said authoritatively.

As Pete started up the car, he said, "You've got really great parents, Donna. I like the way you can talk things out with them."

"So do I. No deep, dark secrets in our family."

"I like the way they act to each other. I mean, it's hard for me to realize they've been married . . . how many years?"

"Twenty-two," Donna said. "I know what you mean. My mother and father are about the best married couple I know."

"Yeah, like we'll be someday," Pete said meaningfully.

It frightened Donna when Pete spoke like that. They had only been dating since September, yet Pete often acted as if they were engaged. Which was very upsetting, since she felt there was an enormous difference between them. It hadn't been that apparent at first.

When they had first met, they frequently had taken picnic lunches along the shore of the Potomac. In the sweet autumn air, with boats going up and down the river and Donna's guitar accompanying them, they had sung all the songs they both liked and that Donna could play — Bob Dylan, Paul Simon, Joan Baez, Joni Mitchell. They both laughed at the same things. While Pete came from a hardworking Pennsylvania farm family and Donna from a well-to-do professional one, their taste in music, films, and other contemporary things was close.

What bothered Donna was that she felt these things were superficial. As a person, she was so much more analytical than Pete. She loved — almost couldn't help — wondering what made people behave the way they did. Pete, on the other hand, was completely disinterested in the subject. People were the way they were.

Pete had always wanted to be an athletic coach. What a different occupation from a psychologist! More than that, Donna was disturbed by Pete's basically old-fashioned ideas. While he said he admired the way her mother had been able to run a home and raise a family while she practiced medicine, Donna suspected that it was not the way Pete would actually want it himself when he was married. A wife's work would be secondary to his own.

"If I can't be me even after I'm married,

I couldn't stand it," she had often said to Janet. "I don't believe I was put on earth just to be a cook, a houseworker, a secretary, and a nursemaid for someone. Sure, I want to get married someday and have babies. But I want to have a career too. Why can't a man and woman share equally in a home and in their jobs?"

"It's not the way the world is," Janet would reply.

"Then let's change the world," was Donna's answer.

What Pete and Donna had very much in common was their strong physical attraction for each other. Now, as Pete parked the car in the driveway adjoining Donna's apartment house and turned off the ignition, Donna wanted and did not want what was about to happen. Pete said in a low husky tone, "Donna," and she felt herself responding wildly to his mood. He took her into his arms, and then with one hand tipped her head back until her lips were nearly touching his. He said once more, "Donna," and then he was kissing her, deeply, with so much feeling it both delighted and frightened her. *We're too young*, she thought. *I'm not sure enough. I'm not sure I want to spend my life with you, Pete, dear as you are.*

She said nothing of this, merely yielded

a moment longer to his kiss and then gently, ever so gently, put her hands up between them and moved away from him.

"I understand," Pete said. "Don't worry, Donna."

They said good night and he drove off. Donna thought, *But I do worry, Pete. This is getting much more serious than I can handle.*

Still, the last thing she thought of before she fell asleep that night was Janet. Janet lying in the hospital, badly injured. Janet wanting, needing to know who she was, where she came from.

I don't know what the next step is, Donna thought. But I'll find out for Janet. I'm going to go ahead without her. No one is going to stop me.

Chapter 6

It hadn't been easy getting the daffodils, not at this time of year. Their yellow spriteliness lit the corridor of University Hospital as Donna searched for Room 521. "Ms. Janet Bryson," the small placard on the door read. Donna smiled. "Ms." was at last making itself felt as the accepted form of address, if a sedate institution like this was using it.

She tapped with her fingernails lightly on the door till she heard a faint "Come in." Inside the room, a white-clad nurse stood beside the bed. Donna was appalled by Janet's appearance. There were blue and green and yellow bruises on her cheeks and on her jaws, and her nose was swollen grossly. Her eyes were small puffed slits between the eyelids; they looked out at Donna listlessly. Her entire head was bandaged right down to the eyebrows.

"Are you related to the patient?" the nurse asked.

Donna said quickly, "No, but I'm her best friend. I only came to bring her these" — indicating the flowers. Janet said nothing, didn't smile, didn't move, just looked out at Donna from behind those puffs of bruised flesh.

"The patient is not to be disturbed in any way." The nurse took the flowers from Donna's outstretched hands. "I'm sure she appreciates your bringing her these. But I don't think you should stay."

Donna looked at Janet. "Want me to stay a moment, Janet?"

The nurse said, "Oh, no, you can't stay. I'm sorry."

Noticing that the nurse was holding a pile of crumpled linen and a tray of soiled dishes, Donna said, "I'm sorry, Janet. She says I have to go." But she winked broadly at her friend.

The nurse explained as Donna left the room with her, "Her jaw is so badly damaged, she can't speak without great pain. She's better off without company."

Donna waited until the nurse turned down the corridor, then she reentered the room. Her mother had sometimes spoken about officious nurses who overstepped their bounds and acted like stern overseers rather than ministers to the sick. This nurse was like that.

Donna entered the room unobtrusively and touched Janet's hand gently. Janet turned her head, and in a moment her eyes filled with tears.

Donna said softly, "Oh, darling. Darling Janet. Is it that bad? What can I do for you?"

Janet did not utter a sound or make a single move. Donna noticed the small bed table which held a glass of water and a small box of face tissues. Below the formica top there was a drawer. Donna opened it and saw inside the familiar manila folder. "In The Matter Of The Adoption Of Janet Bryson." Then Donna remembered — it had been in Janet's briefcase last night when she was attacked. She had been carrying it around with her ever since they'd come back from their fruitless journey to The Perry Home and City Hall, while they were still trying to figure out their next move.

"This is great," Donna said, holding up the folder. "Now I can go ahead while you're here getting well. How about that?"

Again silence. And a sad, sad look on that poor damaged face.

From outside Donna heard the nurse's footsteps. She said hastily, "Don't worry

73

about a thing, Jan. You just concentrate on getting well. Mother says everything is A-okay, nothing serious. You can be up and out of here in a week or so."

She couldn't stand the terrible look of depression on Janet's face. She touched Janet's hand ever so gently and said, "I'm going to get a real lead, Janet. I promise I will, even if it means that I have to take apart The Perry Home *and* Mrs. Fitch to find it."

Janet slowly, painfully shook her head. Her lips started to move and Donna bent over to hear when the nurse charged angrily into the room.

"What is the meaning of this? I told you you weren't allowed to stay."

Donna held up the folder. "I came back to get this — it's my homework."

She looked at Janet, hoping to see her smile, but the swollen eyelids were closed over the eyes; Janet either hadn't heard or didn't care.

The nurse followed Donna closely and this time watched to see her get on the elevator.

It was when she was walking back across the campus that frustration overcame her. Janet was obviously in no mood to cope with anything. She must talk to her mother about Janet's state of mind. Sure, the beating must have shocked her as much as wounded her, if not more. But underneath it, Donna knew there was justification for Janet's despair.

Everything they'd done so far seemed to bear out her father's warning. People were so secretive about adoptions. They almost acted as if they wanted to hold back an investigation. Look at Mrs. Fitch. Look at the clerk at City Hall, implying that they would never be able to discover Janet's true identity.

I'm really stuck, she thought. Maybe I've taken on something I have no right to get involved with. What do I do now?

She saw the paper poking out of the mailbox down in the lobby as she started off to school with her book bag slung across her shoulder. Donna's mail was usually unexciting, since family and friends lived in Philadelphia and there was little reason for people to write her. But this was different. The pale blue envelope had a return address in the corner: "P. Chapman, Box 348, Baltimore, Maryland."

She ripped the envelope open with impatient fingers; her heart leaped as she read the words:

"Here's a new piece of information that may help you. The State Department of Welfare, Adoption Reports Section, keeps a registry of all adoptions. I snooped around The Perry Home and found they *do* have a file on Janet Bryson — *and* the Welfare Department has the document file on the case. Best of all — it is not sealed; it is open to public inspection . . ."

When she finished reading the note, Donna gave a little shriek and kicked up her heels in an impromptu joyous jig. A couple of girls in the lobby grinned at her antics, but the housemother looked at her reprovingly.

"It's all right," Donna assured her. "It's a letter from my husband. He says he and our five children are fine. The oldest boy's wife just had triplets. I'm a grandmother!"

The housemother shook her head in disapproval as Donna skipped out the door. In her day, students behaved much more.

Donna's first stop after class was the gymnasium. There in the huge vaulted glass-roofed gym, she found Pete coaching some young boys and girls in basic karate techniques. The children's ages ranged from nine or ten to fourteen; they were from the settlement house on Pitt Street, in the poorer section of town. The kids all stared at her as Pete walked over to welcome her.

"Donna, you're just in time to help me with my demonstration." He pulled her over to the children.

"Now, wait," Donna said.

"Folks, this is Donna Rockford." The kids looked at her curiously. "She's going to show you how easy it is to do the grip I was telling you about."

Donna said, "You know I don't know a thing about karate, Pete."

"All the better," he said. "What I want to do is show how someone much lighter than an attacker can throw him for a loop."

The children's eager faces were waiting; she couldn't disappoint them.

"Okay," she said. "But you've got to do me a favor afterwards. Promise?"

"I promise, I promise. Now, come on."

In a few minutes he had shown her how to fend off an attack made from behind. She seized his outstretched right hand and, following his orders exactly, twisted, lifted, and threw. He landed on his back on the mat as the kids applauded wildly.

"Remember," Pete said when it was quiet again, "we only use karate tech-

niques when we're being attacked by someone. It isn't always possible to get a
proper grip."

"What do you do if that happens?" a
bright-eyed youngster asked.

"That's a good question," Pete said.
"What you do then is anything you can.
Anything. Anyone who's attacking you
means business. Go for his throat, if you
can." He tapped his adam's apple, his
windpipe. "Cut off the air in his windpipe,
and you give yourself a couple of seconds
that can help you escape."

Donna thought, He's such a good
teacher. He knows these kids live in the
slums and he's making sure they learn
some lessons for survival. She was very
proud of him.

"Never play games with karate," Pete
was saying. "Plenty of people have been
badly hurt fooling around like that. But
when you need it, karate is a terrific
weapon. If you can't use it properly during
an attack, use what you've got. That's the
main thing . . . *use what you've got.*"

The hour bell rang and after the kids
had left, Pete said, "All right, talk."

In a rush, Donna spilled out her plan.
"I can't wait to go down to Baltimore to
visit that Department of Welfare, Pete,"
she said.

"You may be getting yourself excited about nothing," he said. "Remember what happened the last time you went to Baltimore."

"But this is different. Pamela Chapman saw how disappointed we were. And she's not the type to stir us up again over nothing." She hesitated. "What I want to know is — can you drive me down?"

"Sure," he said. "When would you like to go?"

"Now," she said.

"And cut classes? Just like that?"

"I've only got Russian History and Medieval Music. I'm probably flunking the first one, so one class won't hurt, and at this point I really know more about Medieval Music than I wish to know."

"You've never flunked anything. You're much smarter than I am — and that could become a problem between us." Pete stopped. He saw that she was in no mood for jokes. "Can you be ready in a half hour?"

"Oh, Pete! Of course!" She was ecstatic.

It was in moments like these that Donna felt her future was not really in her own hands. She could never resist Pete when he was kind and loving to her. Someplace in there was the key to some deep inner feelings; she didn't know exactly what they were. And this was no time to examine them. She and Pete were not what mattered right now. Janet was the one they had to think of.

The Department of Welfare in Baltimore was in an ancient and once very impressive huge stone building. The office they were sent to was depressing, with its dirty green walls in need of paint and ugly scarred wooden benches and chairs too hard for comfort. But the middle-aged man at the desk was friendly, and he seemed anxious to help.

"There's no problem. If you wish to look up the records of your adoption, Miss, all you'll need is some identification."

For a moment, Donna hesitated. How had she been misled? Pamela Chapman's note had clearly said, "Open to public inspection." I've been a fool, Donna thought. I thought it meant any public person. Maybe it does, but I'm not going to take any chances.

She pulled the folder from The Perry Home out of the briefcase and handed it to the man.

"Hmmm . . . Bryson, Janet Bryson," he said. "Came from The Perry Home, eh?" Donna simply smiled and said nothing. "It certainly is gratifying to see how well you young people who got adopted turn out. I see a lot of you youngsters," he said in a friendly manner. "Especially lately. Seems like everyone is wanting to find out where they came from. You just follow me." He rose from his chair. "We won't keep you in suspense any longer."

Donna cast a look back at Pete, who was sitting on a bench studying his chemistry textbook. She waved and followed the clerk out of the room. He led the way to a small room with several microfilm cameras lined up against the side wall, each in a separate booth.

"Sit there," he said. "I'll be back in a moment." Donna sat down in the first booth.

He was as good as his word. Almost immediately he came into the room with a broad smile on his face. "Here you are, Miss Bryson. But remember, this microfilm will show only a partial record of your past. Don't get your hopes up too high," he warned. "Usually there's a lot missing. But I think you will find at least a few things that can be helpful."

"Thank you," Donna said. She waited while he showed her how to thread the microfilm onto the machine, and then he left.

Donna could hardly control her excitement as she started the film off. In the bright light of the projector she suddenly saw it, *"Report of the Commissioner's Investigation Regarding the Adoption of Janet Willins."*

Willins. Janet's real name!

Janet Willins. Funny, they had never changed her first name. Then Donna realized why. Since Janet had been adopted at ten months of age, she was already used to her first name and they probably had not wanted to upset her psychologically by suddenly calling her by a different name.

The family name, "Willins," was about all the useful information Donna could pick up from the microfilm. There was no mention of Janet's real parents; no light was shed on anything previous to the moment that she had been brought to The Perry Home for adoption.

Donna hurried outside and arranged for a copy of the record, then went back to Pete. "Let's go," she said. "Wait'll you hear the news."

When she told him, he said, "Fantastic! Now all Janet has to do is find out where the Willins family is living."

Donna tugged at his sleeve. "Pete, you dream! That gives me an idea! Come on, we have to find a guard!"

As they took the elevator downstairs, she explained, "This is a municipal building, right? So they must have a place here where they have phone books . . . from Baltimore and Washington." She paused, then her green eyes glinted excitedly. "And New York and Philadelphia and . . ."

"Gotcha," Pete said. "Nice going."

Downstairs they cornered a friendly guard, who said, "Sure thing." He pointed to a corner of the huge lobby. "They've got all kinds of phone books right over there."

They thanked him and ran to the row of phone booths, between which there was an over-sized wooden stand holding many telephone directories. Donna thrust one directory at Pete. "It's the Baltimore book. Look 'Willins' up in that. I'll take Washington, okay, Watson?"

"Okay, Holmes." They both laughed and dug into the directories.

Minutes later, Donna looked up from hers. "Nothing here, Pete. Any luck with yours?"

"Nope. Not a single Willins listed in Washington or any of the suburbs around it. What next?"

She indicated the other books. "As long as we're here, let's see if there's any Willins family in whatever city there's a phone book for. You start at that end, I'll start here."

Fifteen minutes later, they had run through all the directories — covering many of the major cities of the United States. Pete shook his head.

"Well, that's it," he said, shaking his head, discouraged. "Another dead end, baby."

"So what else is new?" Donna brushed her long brown hair impatiently, flinging it back over her shoulder. "Everyone said it's a lot tougher job than anyone would expect."

She lapsed into silence on the ride back to school, her long lashes veiling her eyes as she sat lost in deep thought. Once or twice she sighed heavily.

Finally Pete said, "Listen, don't let it get you down. At least Janet knows her real name. That means somewhere, someplace she can find out who her real folks are."

"Not necessarily," Donna said. Then, on seeing Pete's bewildered look, she explained, "It could be her mother's name."

Pete nodded. "What you're saying is, maybe her mother wasn't married."

"Right, Pete. Willins could be her mother's maiden name. After all, why would a young girl ever give her baby up for adoption? Because probably she wasn't married and her parents wouldn't let her keep the baby. It's still that way today, in lots of cases. And Janet's mother had her nineteen years ago — when people were a lot stricter than today."

Pete pursed his lips. "It must have been pretty rough on a young mother. I mean, if she wanted to keep her baby."

Donna nodded. "It must have been awful!"

"I wonder if that's how it was with Janet's mother," Pete said speculatively.

"If we keep on," Donna said, "we'll find her. And when we do, she'll tell Janet the whole story."

Pete said, "Well, let's get back to Philadelphia and tell Janet what we know. Maybe it'll cheer her up."

"I hope so," Donna said fervently. "She needs it."

It was seven o'clock when they arrived. They hurried through the corridors of the hospital and up to Janet's room, where Pete said, "You go in — I want to get some water."

Donna entered the room and saw that Janet was not alone. An orderly stood at her bedside, wearing a white cap and a face mask tied in back covering his nose and mouth. Beside him was a wagon with a tray of small white paper cups on it. Janet did not see Donna come in. She was sitting up, disinterestedly watching television. Some rock band was playing loud music, and the orderly, half-turned away from the door, did not hear Donna come in. He handed a small paper cup to Janet, who took a huge red capsule out of it and with difficulty began to insert it between her lips.

In the doorway, Donna stood watching the tableau with an uneasy feeling. Something was wrong, wasn't it? But what? Then suddenly, as Janet finally got the capsule into her mouth, Donna yelled, "Don't take that, Janet! Spit it out!"

In the same instant, the orderly spun around and ran past them and out the door.

"Get him!" Donna shouted at Pete, who had just come into the room.

"Get who?" Pete asked.

"That orderly. He's a fake! Get him!" Donna said.

Donna watched Pete run out into the corridor, then she hurried to Janet's bedside. On the white coverlet, the huge red capsule, moistened from having been partly in Janet's mouth, was leaving a deep, wine-red stain. Donna took a tissue from the box on the bed table, gingerly lifted the red capsule into it, and carefully wrapped it up.

Janet was looking at her in astonishment.

"How did I know he was a phony?" Donna asked. Janet nodded. "What started me thinking was watching you try to put this huge pill in your mouth. Your jaw is still so sore you can't eat solid food or even talk without having pain. Then why would any doctor give you such a big thing to swallow?" She added firmly, "Certainly not my mother. There are almost no medicines that you can't administer in liquid form." Janet nodded, and Donna continued, "So when the capsule started me thinking, I took a good look at him. That was when I noticed what was wrong with his appearance. I really saw it the moment I came into the room, but I made no connection at the time."

She paused for a moment, then as Janet looked questioningly at her, she said, "I should have realized the very first minute that he was no real orderly. He was dressed all in white — white cap, white gown — and yet underneath his gown he was wearing perfectly pressed navy-blue trousers and navy-blue patent leather shoes with gold link chains. The uniform in this hospital usually calls for white shoes, but even when they're not, they *must* be rubber-soled shoes — with no metal on them. Metal creates friction in the operating room and is both a fire and electric-shock hazard."

At that moment, Pete entered the room, out of breath from running. "Whoever that guy was, he disappeared in a flash. Half the nurses and orderlies are looking for him right now, going up and down staircases, all over the place, but I don't think they'll find him, not in that uniform, not in a hospital this big. He must be out of the building by now."

"Too bad. He must be the same one who's been after Janet." Donna said to Janet directly, "The one who probably put you in the hospital."

Pete said, "What made you suspect him, Donna? He looked perfectly fine to me."

When Donna had filled him in on the story, he said, "What about the face mask he was wearing?"

"That meant very little by itself, Pete. Sometimes hospitals like their orderlies to wear them when the orderly has a cold, or when there's a flu or virus epidemic around. Like now. Mother says she's been getting very little sleep because of the flu cases she's been called out on."

Pete said, "I've got to give you points for all that deduction, Donna. None of it would have occurred to me."

"I'm a doctor's daughter," Donna said. "But we have news for Janet, don't we, Pete?" He winked at her and she went over to Janet, took her hand, and said. "You're someone's daughter, too. Not only the Brysons', Janet."

Despite the pain, Janet tried to speak — it came out in a mumble: "Oo 'oun 'ow?"

"You found out?" Donna decoded. "Yes, I found out. Now hold yourself together, Janet. Here comes your last name. Are you ready for it?"

This time Janet didn't speak, but nodded her head vigorously.

"Willins. W-I-L-L-I-N-S. Janet Willins — that's the name you were born with, baby." Then she added, "Your mother's name was Ellen Willins."

Janet sat there motionless. She closed her eyes, while Donna held her hand, squeezed it, then bent over to pat Janet's cheek ever so gently. A small tear began to run slowly down the cheek, but when Janet opened her eyes, there was in them a look of incredible joy.

Donna kissed her and said, "Now all you've got to do is get well, fast. My mother told me your concussion is ever so much better, and so is the ankle. I'll find out how long it will be before you can get up and out of here."

Janet said, " 'un 'eek."

"One week?" Donna said.

" 'Es," Janet said.

Donna thought, it's working. She's starting to come out of it. She's even speaking better. She said, "Okay, don't talk any more, we can't have you speechless when you get out." Janet giggled and Donna said, "Because we're really going to get this investigation moving fast once you're discharged. Mother says you'll be able to go right about your business. Are you ready for it?"

Janet grinned and nodded her head "yes" several times.

"I wonder who that man is who keeps trying to get to Janet?" Donna said to Pete in the car.

"Whoever he is, he means business. Someone's got to watch over Janet from here on out, and someone's got to watch over you."

"Why me?"

"Because you're Janet's best friend. Because you live together. It's possible he's getting more and more angry because you keep getting in his way," Pete said sternly.

"Okay. I'll admit there's danger." She touched his arm tenderly. "And I appreciate your concern, Pete, really I do. Only, trust me a little; I'm not an idiot." She reached into her purse and took out the white tissue that held the red capsule. "Please take me to my house, Pete. I want to show Mother this medication and ask her what it is. That is, if it's okay with you?"

"Sure." He bent down and kissed her lightly, then swung the car down Chestnut Street heading south. "It's almost dinnertime," he said. "Do you suppose I'll be able to get a piece of cheese or something?"

"You won't have to hint to my mother. You know her," Donna said, smiling. "She's got enough for five extra people every time we sit down at the groaning board."

"Can't wait," Pete said. "I'm starving."

Tonight the table *was* a groaning board. A huge standing rib roast of beef — crackly on the outside, juicy and savory on the inside, was the center of a large platter decorated with small roast potatoes, fresh asparagus, tiny Belgian candied carrots, and in a heavy silver tureen, thick brown gravy.

"Delicious! Dr. Rockford, this is the best roast beef I ever ate in my life," Pete

said, unaware that he made a similar pro-
nouncement every time he ate at the Rockfords'. It was always the best turkey, the
best roast pork, the best beef stew, the
best lobster bisque, the best anything he
had ever eaten in his life.

During the meal, there was only light
dinner conversation. The Rockfords rarely
discussed upsetting or controversial matters during mealtime; they all had too
much love and respect for good food well-
prepared.

But after dinner, when the family was
all gathered in front of the fireplace in
the living room, drinking coffee, Donna's
father took over. "Your mother has arranged for Janet's room to be watched
more carefully. And the hospital is tighten-
ing up all-over security as well, she informs
me. A perfect stranger should not just
be able to walk into a patient's room and
do what he wants."

"How did you know?" Donna said to
her mother.

"My dear daughter — Janet is my patient, remember? The first thing they did
was call me."

"This is what he was trying to get
Janet to take." Donna handed the tissue
with the red capsule to her mother.

Dr. Rockford examined it carefully.

Then she said, "I can't be sure, but it looks like a tranquilizer that's manufactured by Case and Farber." She loosened the top of the capsule and put it to her nose. "This is weird," she announced.

"Why weird?" her husband said.

"It smells like bitter almonds — which would indicate cyanide, of course. But cyanide in this dosage could kill a horse."

"Maybe that's what it was intended to do," her husband said.

"What I'm trying to say is that I think this is a type of medication they dose animals with. When I visited the veterinary college last year, I think it was used on a steer. I'll have it analyzed," she said.

Donna's father took over then. "In all conscience, we must ask you not to get any further involved in this matter," he said. "I intend to have a talk with Janet and ask her to do the same — drop the investigation for the time being. If she doesn't agree, I feel I will have to notify Mrs. Bryson in Florida."

"Dad, no! You don't know how much this means to Janet. I've never seen her as upset as she's been since her father died." She paused. "Her schoolwork has fallen off; she may even flunk out, did you know that? If we give up now, I don't know what she'll do."

"I agree with Donna, Paul," her mother said. "If Janet is determined to have this information — and I understand her need — you can't stop her. She should be made aware of the danger she faces if she continues. Then, if she decides to go ahead, it is her responsibility. She's not a child — she's a fully grown young woman."

"And so am I, Mother," Donna said gravely. "Would you want me to promise you I'll stop helping her and then break that promise? We've never operated that way."

Donna looked at both her parents watchfully. Her father spoke first: "What's your next step? I mean, if your mother and I do agree with what you're saying."

"Frankly, Dad, I don't know. If the adoption home and the City Hall refuse to cooperate — and they have — I don't know what we can do next." Donna sounded dispirited. "I never should have promised Janet anything. I really don't know what I'm doing."

Her father looked at her mother, who nodded, and then he said to Donna, "I have a suggestion. Frankly, I'm not an expert on the adoption laws of Maryland. But my firm has, as you know, a remarkable law library. You can research the whole subject of adoption there, Donna. John

94

Harbaugh will be glad to help you. Maybe you can come up with something to give you your next direction."

Donna realized that her father — while trying to be helpful — actually hoped to divert her from further physical action by opening the door to research; it would take a lot of time, especially for someone like herself, who knew nothing at all about law.

So they had reached a Mexican stand-off. The kind of compromise that grinds the wheels of progress to a halt.

She had no alternative but to accept.

Tomorrow she would invade her father's law library. What happened next would be in the lap of the gods.

It wasn't easy running from class to the law library then back to class, back to the library, then back home to study. But that was the dizzy schedule that Donna was operating on. Janet would be home on Friday. What Donna wanted was to be able to tell Janet the next step in the investigation.

It was a long, grueling week, but in the end it paid off. What she came up with was the possibility of going to the court through which Janet had been adopted. That court should have somewhere a final order of adoption. And on that final order they might find the names of both Janet's parents, and some further clues to Janet's background.

She took the problem to John Harbaugh.

"Is this right?" she asked. "Is there anything that says people can't see a final order of adoption?"

"Not to my knowledge," John admitted. "But I don't see how you could be shown it without Janet being there."

"Don't worry. Thanks for everything, John. Next stop — the courthouse in Baltimore."

Chapter 7

It was a cold but beautifully sunny day when Janet, using a cane for support, came hobbling down the steps of University Hospital.

"You look like you've been walking with a cane for years," Donna told her. "Isn't it hard to do?"

"Not after you've been lying in bed cooped up in a hospital room for two weeks," Janet answered. She took several deep breaths of the fresh December air. "Mmm, now I know what they mean when they say the air was like wine."

"Cold wine," Donna said.

"Whatever it is, I think I'm getting drunk from it."

As they went down the flagstone walk which had been cleared of snow, Janet's face broke into a huge smile. "It's like hitting yourself over the head with a hammer — it feels so good when you stop. Know what I mean?"

"What you're saying is that if you're feeling depressed, check into a hospital for a little while. Then check out. Right?"

"Right."

By the time they got into the car, they were in the best of spirits.

"Where shall we go for lunch?" Janet asked. "I'm starved."

Donna reached behind her and pulled a tan canvas knapsack off the seat and handed it to Janet. "Where we're going to eat is — here." Then, seeing the look of disappointment on Janet's face, she added, "We've got to get down to the courthouse in Baltimore before four o'clock."

"What for?"

"You'll see. I don't want to get your hopes up, but someone who should know thinks that today we could hit the jackpot."

Janet said, pleading, "Donna! Please don't be mysterious. It's not your style and besides . . ."

"Shut up and eat," Donna said. "I went to a great deal of trouble to get all your favorite junk food, sparing no expense."

"Bologna sandwiches!" Janet shrieked as she poked through the carton. "And pickles! Cole slaw, potato chips, olives!

Chocolate eclairs! Donna, you're a dream. After all that yecchy hospital food . . ."

"We'll be sorry later when we're both sick to our stomachs in the courthouse, and throw up in front of a judge."

"It's worth it," Janet said, biting into a huge juicy pickle.

The miles sped by. At two o'clock the red Mustang braked to a halt in a parking lot near the courthouse.

Inside, Donna spoke to the clerk in charge of adoptions. "What we would like is to see a certain order of adoption. We believe it's here someplace."

"We do have the final order of adoption — at least in most cases. But we couldn't possibly let you see it unless the adoptee were here," the man said.

But Donna was, after all those hours spent in the law library, pretty certain of her ground. "This is Janet Bryson, the adoptee. She came from The Perry Home originally. We have already learned her mother's maiden name — Ellen Willins."

The man looked uncertainly at Janet. "You have identification?" She nodded, and pulled her driver's license out of her wallet.

He was still staring at it when Donna said with authority, "We have very little time, sir. I have to get back to my father's law office in Philadelphia. He's very interested in Miss Willins' case."

That did it. "Come this way," the man said.

The girls followed him to a big, academic-looking room not unlike one of the study halls at school. The man left the room and then came back, holding the by-now familiar yellow manila file folder.

"Your name is at the end of the alphabet, practically," he said to Janet. "Makes it easier to find than some of the rest. We have records here going back fifty, sixty years, you know."

Donna asked where they could make copies of the records.

"You just bring them to me, young lady, and I'll see that you get copies," he said.

The two girls opened the folder and started going through the papers almost feverishly.

Then Donna found it. *The* paper. The one that told them unmistakably: Janet was indeed illegitimate. Under the heading, "Father," there was listed, "Johnson, first name unknown — not contributing to support of child."

Donna held the paper, just staring at it, not knowing what to do. Which was silly, she knew, because Janet would have to see it. Even now, Janet was looking at her, waiting. It was so embarrassing. The fact of Janet's being illegitimate meant nothing to Donna. Janet was Janet, no matter who or where she had come from. But holding on to the paper that way somehow was giving it more importance than it actually had. Donna cursed her tactlessness.

Janet quietly took the paper and just as quietly read it, her face revealing nothing. After a long while, she said, "Did you see, Donna? I mean where it says, 'Mother's age'? She was only eighteen years old, my mother — a year younger than I am now."

Donna touched her friend's hand. "It's sad, when you think of how hard it must have been for her."

Janet said, "It must have been awful. Look how much freer people are in their thinking today, and yet it's still a terrible shock to parents when their unmarried daughter tells them she's going to have a baby. Think of what it must have been nineteen years ago, in 1958, for my mother."

"Terrible," Donna said. "The poor woman."

A young man writing at the other end of the long table looked up in annoyance at them.

101

"Let's go," Janet said in a whisper. "I want to get a copy of all this."

Back at the man's desk, it took only a few minutes before he returned with the copies Janet had asked for. "If I can help you in any way," he said to Donna, "be sure to let me know."

"What beats me," Donna said as they pulled away from the crowded courthouse in their car, "is how people respond to the threat of authority. Mention that you have a lawyer for a father and look what happens." She was trying to divert Janet from her very heavy thoughts, but she wasn't succeeding. "Want me to shut up?" she asked.

"No, no. But I have a lot to think about, Donna."

Donna stopped the car and Janet asked in surprise, "Why are we stopping here?"

"You need time," Donna said. "For heaven's sake, you've just gotten the most important information anyone could have. You're beginning to find out who you are. We can't just drive back to school."

"What else is there to do?"

"I don't know. What I'd like to do is go to The Perry Home."

"What's the point of that?"

"I'm not sure. But for one thing, I'd like

102

to tell Mrs. Fitch what we've learned. Then she might 'remember' more about your case."

They were both excited when they entered The Perry Home this time. In the cheery green and yellow room, Pamela Chapman was typing away at a small desk; she was strangely cool to them. "Do you want me to get Mrs. Fitch for you?"

She had hardly spoken when Mrs. Fitch herself walked in. Pamela Chapman might be behaving differently to them, but the matron was her same old self — coolly disapproving.

"This *is* a surprise. I didn't think I'd be seeing either of you again." She added in a falsely sweet tone, "Especially you, Miss Bryson."

Donna said, just as sweetly, "Bryson — or Willins." Then at the blank look in Mrs. Fitch's eyes, "That's her real name, you know. Willins."

Mrs. Fitch didn't bat an eyelash as she seated herself in the armchair behind her desk. "Oh, I know that. You see, I actually found the entire file while you were here on your first visit."

Donna said, "How could you? How could you do such a thing to anyone?"

Mrs. Fitch smiled coldly. "Actually, I

never expected her to find out her real name. You both have a lot of persistence," she said grudgingly.

"Why wouldn't I have?" Janet said. "Anyone would want to know what I'm trying to find out about myself. Anyone would want to know who she really is, where she really came from, who her real mother was," she said hotly.

"Well, I don't approve of it," Mrs. Fitch said sternly. "All you're going to do is stir up a lot of trouble. Why don't you think of your poor mother? How about her? If you do find her, and if she's alive, which she may not be — girls like that often lead *very* irregular lives. Well, there's no doubt in my mind she won't want to see you. Maybe she's married now."

Janet suddenly stood up. "Look, I don't want you talking that way about my mother! You have no right to speak of any woman that way, just because she had a child when she wasn't married." Her eyes filled with angry tears.

Mrs. Fitch retorted, her voice high-pitched, "I will get you the file — but I warn you, you won't find anything important in it." She turned and smiled silkily at Pamela. "Get them the Willins' file, my dear. The sooner they get what they want and leave, the sooner we can go back to our work."

Pamela, her eyes cool and uncommunicative, glanced briefly at the girls. "Certainly, Mrs. Fitch. I'll be right back."

But when she returned with the papers, she said to Mrs. Fitch, "I'm afraid I have to leave now. I'm expecting dinner company."

"Certainly, dear," Mrs. Fitch said sweetly.

Donna could not believe what she was hearing. Could this be happening? Pamela and Mrs. Fitch friends?

But they quickly turned their attention to the folder Mrs. Fitch handed them. There was very little in it. Nothing important. Not a thing that they didn't already know.

Mrs. Fitch, watching closely, noted their disappointment and said acidly, "I told you. Nothing. Now if you'll take my advice, you'll give this up." She shook a warning finger at Janet. "You can bring terrible shame down on your mother's head. She's never told anyone about you, you can be sure of that. I think you should drop this whole matter right here. *I* personally will do nothing to encourage you."

Donna said, "Thanks a lot. Your advice and your encouragement mean exactly zero. We found the name of her real parents without your help. We are going to continue our search." Beside her, Janet nodded vigorously. "And I plan to speak to my father, an attorney, about officials in children's homes who try to block investigations because they're prejudiced. He may be able to stir up a little action to correct the condition."

Both girls were unprepared for Mrs. Fitch's reaction. Her hand settled on a heavy marble ashtray and a blaze of pure hatred crossed her face momentarily. It was terrifying. But then she regained control.

"Good day," she said calmly. "And if I were you, I'd be sure to phone in advance if you plan to return. We have a very crowded schedule, as you have seen, and I am not at all sure when we will be able to fit you in again. I'm sure you understand."

"We certainly do," Donna said. "Goodbye, Mrs. Fitch."

When they were outside, Janet said, "You scared me, Donna. She's such a crazy lady I thought she was going to throw that marble ashtray or something at us," she said.

Janet had that worried, depressed expression on her face again; that was what prompted Donna to say as they reached the car, "We're going to the Monmouth Inn and staying over tonight. Got that?"

"We certainly are not," Janet said. "It costs a fortune."

"Eighteen dollars is not a fortune," Donna said. "I'll treat us. I have the money in my purse."

Janet reached over and closed the purse Donna had opened. "It's not just eighteen dollars. We have to eat, don't we? And I know why you put that money aside . . . to buy some games for Pete's kids from the settlement house, right?" Donna said nothing. "I may have sunk low, Donna, but not low enough to deprive those already deprived kids of their presents."

"You're right," Donna said. "I'm out of my mind. I just don't know the next move."

But when she had started up the car and driven slowly along the elm-lined street, the next move was taken care of. It stood there in the form of Pamela Chapman, who stepped out from behind a tree and waved widely at them. Donna braked hastily and the car skidded to the side of the road. Just as quickly, Pamela got to the car.

"Quick! Before she sees us." Pamela

cast a fearful look back at the building they had come from.

Donna raced the motor and the car sped toward the center of town. Pamela's sudden appearance was puzzling, but she relaxed as they left The Perry Home behind and explained: "Listen, you two. I think I may be on to something."

"Pamela, I certainly hope so. We need a boost," Donna said.

"It's nothing specific. Nothing I can lay my hands on. But I think Mrs. Fitch is up to something." Pamela stopped and thought. "If this all sounds fuzzy, well it is. But Mrs. Fitch is having these . . . well, secret phone conversations all the time now with someone. I don't know who. And it may be nothing. Maybe she's got a crazy husband locked up somewhere." She laughed self-consciously. "I told you it was nothing, probably. The thing is, she's never friendly to anyone, but she's being a lot ruder than usual to you two. I don't know why."

"Maybe it's because she really doesn't like us," Janet said.

"I think it's more than that," Donna said.

"That's how I felt." Pamela's voice was conspiratorial. "So I tried to play it smart. Mrs. Fitch and I have never liked each other, not from the first. But I decided it was time we got friendly. You know, it's hard to snoop around if someone doesn't like you."

Donna said, "You mean that your friendliness back there was phony?"

"Right on," Pamela said. "I've been buttering her up so much this last week, it turns my stomach. But it works."

"It does?" Donna asked.

"Yes," Pamela said. "About a week ago she got another phone call and started whispering. It ended with her writing a phone number down on the inside of a case folder. One of the nurses called her and I sneaked a look at the folder open on her desk in front of the phone. Guess whose folder it was," Pamela said gravely. "Janet's case."

Donna whistled softly. "Really?"

Pamela shook her head. "Yes, and I wrote the phone number down." She rummaged in her purse and pulled out a slip. "Not that I had to write it down. I've been calling it for three days and no one answers. Isn't that odd?"

Janet took the piece of paper. "215-863-7544," she read. "What's that?"

"Whoever it is, he's not home. Or she's not home."

"It seems too coincidental," Donna said

109

thoughtfully. "I mean, those mystery phone calls, and the mean way she's treated Janet. Maybe it all fits together somehow. It's got to." She paused. "I owe you an apology, Pamela. Things have gone against us so much I was beginning to think that maybe you and Mrs. Fitch . . ." Her voice trailed off lamely.

"Were working together?" Pamela laughed. "I can't tell you how much I dislike Mrs. Fitch. Women will never get a break in this world until we've changed the minds of females like her. The way she plays up to men. You wouldn't believe it. One minute she's being so awful to any woman who's around, and the moment a man walks in — any man — her personality changes completely. She flatters them so shamelessly, you could throw up."

"I know," Donna said. "I've got a kid sister who acts that way. But she's only sixteen."

"Unsafe at any age," Pamela said.

The three young women laughed in agreement. Then Pamela said, "You ought to see her with the directors of the home. There's one of them — Thomas Wingdale Johnson . . . you'd think royalty was visiting, honestly." Pamela clucked with disgust.

"Johnson?" Janet said. "That's funny."

"What's that about?" Pamela asked.

"Nothing," Janet said. "It's just that it's the same name as my father's."

"Johnson is a common name. There are as many Johnsons as there are Smiths, almost." Pamela grinned. "It's my mother's maiden name — and my middle name — Pamela Johnson Chapman."

"It's Dennis's aunt's name," Janet said. "I just call her 'Mrs. Johnson.' "

"Anyway, Thomas Wingdale Johnson is a big shot. His connection with the home is sort of a hobby," Pamela explained. "He's a political big-shot from Philadelphia. Your city," she said to Donna.

"Why is he connected with a Baltimore children's home?" Donna asked.

"Honey, there are Perry Homes all over the East Coast. He's on the national Board of Directors."

As Donna braked the car at a red light, Pamela said, "Where were you two going when you got into the car?"

"We were having a debate," Donna said. "I wanted to stop over at the same place where we stayed last time we were down here together."

"And I told her no," Janet said.

Pamela looked at Janet and then Donna. "I think you should stay over," she said.

"We really can't af—" Janet began and was stopped by a look from Donna.

"I was a sophomore once myself," Pamela said, grinning. "If you don't mind a lumpy sofa and a sleeping bag, why not stay at my apartment? It's not too far from here," Pamela said.

"What about your dinner guests?" Janet asked.

"Purely imaginary. I just wanted to get out so I could meet you two," Pamela said. "How about it? Really, I'd love to have you."

Donna looked at Janet. No objection there. "We'd love to," she said gratefully.

In a few minutes they were there. Pamela lived in a shabby section of Baltimore; row on row of dilapidated red brick houses with whitewashed but chipped stoops in front lined the block. Children of all kinds frolicked on the pavement, playing batball, riding makeshift skateboards, jumping rope. Several of them clambered around Pamela when she got out of the car. One toothless little child with a lollipop-smeared mouth demanded a kiss; Pamela kissed her, picked her up, and embraced her warmly. It was easy to see that Pamela was a favorite with the junior set on Montaigne Street.

When they got upstairs, Pamela opened

the door on a charming little room. The furniture was shabby in spots, but soft cushions in gay colors were tossed about here and there to lend warmth. It was chilly in the flat; Pamela piled wood into a potbellied stove and lit the fire.

"What a great stove," Janet said.

"It's the real thing," Pamela said. "Look at the date on the side."

Donna and Janet bent down to read the inscription; the date was 1892, and the maker's name was Johnson.

Donna groaned. "Another one."

Everything in the room seemed old, or if new, came from some interesting place. There was a huge bowl filled with odd-shaped shells from a faraway beach in South America. An Indian *serape* was spread on one wall; beneath it a wired old kerosene lamp glowed softly.

Pamela explained, in answer to their questions, "In college I took scholarships and exchange programs wherever I could. So I was in New Mexico one year" — she pointed to the *serape* — "and the next I was down in Peru" — she indicated the shells. "But then in my senior year I volunteered for VISTA and got sent here to this neighborhood." She shrugged. "That did it. I got hooked on the people here. Even if I made enough money to move away and furnish a really fabulous apartment, I couldn't bring myself to do it. This is my home."

Donna said, with admiration, "You've done so much — most people twice your age haven't covered anything like your territory."

Pamela said, "Thanks for the compliment. I think you're about to discover some of my imperfections." She opened the refrigerator and took out some chopped meat, salad, vegetables, and crescent rolls. "What I am not is a good cook. I can manage to keep body and soul together, but that's all. I really don't like cooking."

Donna said, "Let me." At Pamela's questioning look, she explained, "It gives me a chance to think. Peeling potatoes is such a mindless occupation."

"Be my guest," said Pamela, pulling some colorful Mexican dishware out of a cupboard.

A half hour later, as she tasted the poorman's jambalaya — beef and vegetables and gravy on a bed of rice — that Donna had concocted, Pamela said, "Delicious! How do you do it?"

"I'll give you the recipe," Donna said.

"It's no use," Pamela said. "I'll never make it. I hate to cook."

"That's what my father said to my mother," Donna said. "That was twenty-five years ago. Today he's a great cook . . . shoves her out of the kitchen every chance he gets."

"Lots of luck to your father. It's not for me." Pamela said to Janet, "What I'm good at is helping families straighten out problems. The minute we're through eating, tell me how far you've gone and we'll plot the next step."

After they finished dinner and were sitting around sipping hot coffee and eating marshmallow cookies, Pamela said, "Your next step is the city directory. You've got to go and consult it and find out where your mother's family was living, Janet, at the time you were born. Now that you know her name was Ellen Willins, it shouldn't be too difficult."

I hope you're right, Donna thought. I don't think Janet's got strength enough to take too many disappointments.

While she undressed for bed, Donna grew thoughtful. As it became more and more likely that they would be able to locate Janet's mother, she couldn't help thinking, What if the others were right? What if her mother had kept the secret of her birth all these years, married someone else, and had children with her new husband? If so, would she want to see Janet, or would she resent her showing up?

And what about the danger they had already run into? Janet was still hobbling around with a cane from the last attack two weeks ago in Philadelphia.

And what about Mrs. Fitch? What role, if any, was she playing in the mystery they were getting deeper and deeper into?

Chapter 8

After breakfast the next morning, the girls thanked Pamela profusely and insisted on straightening up the apartment. Downstairs they watched Pamela leave for work — stopping off first in a youth center in a delapidated store halfway down the street and then setting out once again for City Hall.

It was there that they ran into problems.

"I'm sorry," the woman in charge of the records department said. "The period that you are looking for, May 17, 1958, is part of a block that we simply have not got all the records on at this time."

"How can that be?" Donna asked. "We're in the right department, aren't we?"

The woman nodded. "You certainly are. But we had a fire about ten years ago — just before we got the microfilm equipment. A clerk happened to leave a small

117

batch of records out on a desk that night. Nothing happened to the papers in the file cabinets; they're metal, of course. But the ones that were left out were the only copies available at that time. We've tried to piece together some sort of material, but it's very sketchy, to say the least."

Janet said to Donna, "Can you believe this? Why did it have to be just the W's that got burned?"

It was then that Donna got her inspiration.

"I wonder," she said. "I wonder, could we possibly see the city records for the year 1940?"

The woman looked at her, puzzled. "Certainly you can. I'll get them."

It was obvious that she thought the request was absurd. Why would anyone want to see the year 1940 when they had come in asking for 1958?

Which was what Janet said. "Why did you ask for 1940?"

"Because that was the year your mother was born. Maybe she was born in Baltimore. If she was, they'll have the records."

"Why couldn't I have thought of that?" Janet said.

"Because you've got so much else on your mind. Do you realize we only started this investigation three weeks ago?"

Janet's eyes lit up. "Maybe three weeks from now we'll know where she is, and I can see her." Her brown eyes sobered. "*If* she wants to see me."

Donna was about to answer when the woman returned, holding a heavy bound volume. She said dubiously, "I don't see how the records of 1940 can be a substitute for the year 1958. I really don't." She indicated a door. "You can use that room."

When they entered the file room next door and sat down at a long walnut table, Janet started flipping the pages of the directory, then stopped. "Here," she said. "You do it. I'm so excited, I'm all thumbs."

Donna took the book from her, and a few seconds later looked up in triumph, her forefinger marking a place in the last pages of the book. "Look! It's here, Janet!"

Janet crowded close to Donna; together they read the entry:

WILLINS, Albert. Wife, Teresa.
83-28 Talbot Street. Occupation —
Fireman. Son, Richard. Daughter,
Ellen.

"Janet! Do you realize what a lead this is?" Donna grabbed her friend's forearm in her enthusiasm. "That's your grandfather's name. And your grandmother's! Isn't it exciting?"

"Yes." Janet hesitated. "But how can it help us if they're not living there any more? How can we find out where they've moved to?" She was beginning to sound despondent.

"Cool it, Janet," Donna said. "One minute you're worried what will happen when you meet your mother, the next you're sure you never will."

"Forgive me," Janet said. "I think I'm crazy."

"You know you're not. I'll admit," Donna said, "that finding people who moved away from a place ten, fifteen years ago is like looking for a needle in a haystack." Her voice suddenly took on a steely edge. "I don't know what's the next move, I really don't. But I promise you that we'll find the right direction to go. We'll find your mother. I know it in my bones."

"I don't know, Donna. I think I'm asking too much of you. And no matter what you say, she may not want to see me at all. Maybe I'll be just too much trouble to her — just like I was when she gave me up nineteen years ago."

"Janet, you've got to stop this negative thinking. We've started on something that you badly want, inside of you, I mean. You know you do. How can we stop now?"

120

Janet said, "You're right. I do want to go on. But meeting my mother isn't the only thing that bothers me. I'm afraid something is going to happen to one or both of us. Especially you. I could never forgive myself if anything bad happened to you."

"Don't even say it," Donna said. "We can't let fear stop us." All the same, she was touched by Janet's obvious concern for her.

Janet said, "I keep thinking, who was that man who attacked me on campus?"

Donna picked up the heavy book as they got up to go. "What bothers me is not who he is, but where he is. That's what I wish we knew."

Neither of them had any way of knowing that they were heading directly into his net.

He struck when they least had reason to expect it.

They had stopped for lunch off Broad Street, and parked their car in a large parking area reserved for the stores in front. They were just getting back in the car in the parking lot. Actually, Donna was preparing to get into the car while Janet waited at the end of the driveway for Donna to turn the car around and pick her up. But as Donna opened her car door, she saw the other one coming. A gray, low-slung sportscar. It was less than fifty feet away. And headed straight for Janet.

Donna shrieked, "Janet!" and she sped toward her friend. In the last moment, as the speeding car was almost upon them, she pushed Janet to the ground and leaped aside herself.

The car sped by in a gray streak. There was no way to see who was behind the wheel. Whoever it was, he — or she — was slumped over the wheel; there was only the single shadow of his presence.

Donna raised herself from the roadway to see if she could glimpse the license number of the car. What she saw was the number "7," then a blur of two numbers, then three letters: "RVD."

She said the number and the letters aloud to herself three times, to set them in her memory. Beside her, Janet was trying to get up, but her lame ankle was a hindrance.

Donna ran over to her and helped her up. "I'm sorry, Janet. Are you hurt?"

"No," Janet said. "But what happened?"

"The phantom strikes again," Donna said, helping her brush off her skirt. "Didn't you see him coming at you?"

"No, I wasn't looking that way. Are you

122

sure it was deliberate? Maybe he just didn't see me."

"Impossible, Janet. Not the way he was driving."

They were back at their car now.

"Someone has definitely been out to get you. First time was when he hurt you and put you in the hospital. The second time was when he tried to give you that capsule. And now he's made his third attempt."

"But you can't be sure about this time," Janet said stubbornly. "It could just have been a reckless kid driving too fast."

"Could be. But my ESP says that it was the same person — or persons — making another try at wiping out Janet Bryson. Why, I don't know. Who? I don't know. But I have got his license plate number — or a big part of it. Two numbers missing. But we'll find him anyway."

"What numbers have you got?"

"Seven, blank, blank, RVD."

"How can they find anyone without the whole license plate number?"

"I don't know. I imagine they run it through computers or something. I'm sure John Harbaugh can help. We'll see. Just relax."

Donna was trying to sound confident, but she didn't feel it. It was a depressed Janet who sat beside her on the ride back to Philadelphia, with Donna driving grimly through the heavily trafficked road. *I'll ask John Harbaugh to get to work on it the minute we get back,* she thought. *We've got to find the lunatic who tried to run her down.*

"I'll do the best I can," John Harbaugh said. "But it will take time."

"How long?" Donna asked.

"Oh, a week or so, I should think."

"No," Donna groaned.

John Harbaugh reached out a hand and tipped it under her chin. "I'll ask them to rush it."

Her eyes lit up as she rose from the chair beside his desk in her father's office. "You are a love, John. I really appreciate it."

"By the way," he said, "your mother left word that you're to call her as soon as you can."

"Thanks, John. I'll call her right away."

He left as she dialed her mother's number.

"I want to see you, dear. It's important," Dr. Rockford said. "Come to the office."

"Sure thing. I'll be right over," Donna said, wondering what it was that made her mother sound so urgent.

* * *

"Sit down, Donna," her mother said, indicating the brown leather chair beside her cherrywood desk.

Her mother's office was a warm room with beige carpeting and muted green walls. Outside, the December wind was lashing against the trees, bringing icy rain and the threat of a blizzard.

"It's about Christmas," her mother said. "Your father has been asked to cover the special convention on International Law in Geneva this year. It's quite an honor, but we'll be away for almost two weeks, starting December 20th."

"Oh, Mother — no! What about Christmas?"

Her mother took Donna's hand. "How would you like to spend part of your Christmas vacation with Janet?"

"How can I?" Donna said. "Janet's going down to Florida to see her mother over Christmas. That is," she added, "if she can get together enough for her fare. She doesn't want to ask her mother for it."

"Your father and I would like to treat you and Janet to the trip down. Our spies have told us there's a round trip charter flight from the University Medical School to Miami. That's only an hour away from Fort Lauderdale. Think you can make it?"

Donna shrieked with pleasure. "Oh,

125

Mother! What a sensational idea. Wait'll I tell Janet. It's just what she needs now. She'll go out of her mind."

She leaped up and gave her mother a hug and kissed her cheek.

"No one, but no one, ever had such parents," she chortled.

"Remember that, will you, the next time you think your father or I are being just too dense about something?" her mother said. But she was pleased by Donna's obvious joy.

"The charter leaves December 24th at noon and returns a week later on the 31st, just in time for you to have New Year's Eve with Pete. Does that suit you?"

Donna said, "I love it. But I'll miss the tree trimming and Christmas dinner and..."

"No you won't," her mother said. "We're going to trim the tree and have all the festivities including Christmas dinner a week earlier. In our house, Christmas Eve will come on December 18th this year."

"Elizabeth, you're a winner. I'm so glad I chose you for a mother."

"We're not really doing it for you, Donna," her mother teased. "We were mostly thinking of Janet — she's so much nicer a person than you are."

"Mother! Enough's enough," Donna said, but she was smiling.

"Janet's had a terrible time this past month. I imagine she'll be delighted to have you with her."

Donna said thoughtfully, "Suppose her mother or her aunt don't have room enough for me?"

Her mother said, "Oh, they have. We've already spoken to them in Florida."

"How did you get their number?" Donna asked.

"The same spies who told us where Pete is planning to take you and Janet on New Year's Eve."

"Oh, where? You know where he's taking me . . . us?" Donna was bursting with curiosity.

"I do indeed. And you can't force the information out of me. Not even with torture. It's Pete's surprise."

"I've got to go and tell Janet," Donna said. "Excuse me, Mother. And thanks a million!"

Janet yelled when she heard the news. "Donna! Are you serious? Do they really mean it?"

"They really mean it."

The two girls were sitting in Pagano's, sharing a plate of steaming lasagna and a big farmer salad. Beside them, Pete sat, eating half a grapefruit.

He said gloomily, "It isn't fair. Here they sit, planning to spend a whole week under the tropical sun lying on a sandy beach, and I'm stuck in the dead of winter in Philadelphia." When the girls turned their attention to him, he said reproachfully, "And as if that's not bad enough, I have to sit with a half a sour grapefruit watching them gorge themselves on pasta."

"You don't *have* to suffer, Pete," Donna said. "But since you want to win the gold medal in Thursday night's exhibition, you'd better get that gorgeous bod down to middleweight shape — 165 pounds, soaking wet. Check?"

"Check," Pete said. "Anyway, you'll be back for New Year's Eve. You're going to love how we're spending it."

"Pete, please." Donna stopped a forkful of food on its way to her mouth. "I can't stand the suspense. What are we doing New Year's Eve?"

"Now it's my turn," Pete grinned maliciously. "My lips are sealed." He wiped his mouth with a napkin, rose, kissed the top of Donna's head, then Janet's, said, "See you," and was gone.

"You're lucky, Donna," Janet said. "You

128

and Pete can see each other so often. I've almost forgotten what Dennis looks like."

"Don't take on so," Donna said. "You'll be seeing him in Florida in exactly ten days. Isn't that super?"

"I'll tell you, Donna," Janet said, "I'm really worried about Dennis."

"Are you kidding?" Donna said. "He's written you at least twice a week since September. And he calls you at least once a week. Didn't he call you again last night?"

"Yes — and that's what worries me. Last night's phone call, I mean. He sounded so — so strange."

"Why?"

"Every time I ask about his mother and father lately, he sort of slides off the subject, fast. He did it last night too."

Donna said, "It's probably your imagination. Besides, you'll be seeing him so soon. If there's something on his mind you can ask him right in person."

"I don't think I'm imagining it. But you're right." Janet sighed and pushed her plate of food away. "There's nothing I can do about it till we get there."

As they walked back to their apartment, an angry snowstorm swirled about them. Donna wished they were already safely down south in Florida.

Chapter 9

The plane soared over the bay and headed downward toward the airport. Below, the myriad lights of Miami Beach twinkled in a multi-colored wonderland. The deep blue waters of the bay soon yielded to the white gleaming airstrips of Miami Airport. In a moment, the voice over the intercom was announcing, "Thank you, ladies and gentlemen, flight number 653 to Miami is now over. We hope you had a pleasant trip and that . . ."

The two young women paid little attention to the Captain's message. They were much too excited. Janet, of course, had been to Florida before, but this was all new to Donna, who was drinking it in eagerly.

The change was apparent the second they stepped off the air-conditioned plane and started down the steps leading to the glassed-in reception area. A wonderful warm wave of tropical air caressed their cheeks. A clump of palm trees, gaily lit with red and pink and orange and pale green lights stood gracefully tall amidst the red poinsetta bushes. Just inside the glass doors of the reception lounge, they saw Dennis waiting. His thick, sandy red hair and tall bronzed figure clad in a white jumpsuit made it easy to pick him out from the crowd. He spotted them and waved wildly as he hurried over.

"Janet!" He swept her up in his arms and held her tight. "Am I glad to see you!"

Donna, watching, felt like a benevolent mother hen beaming on her pet chick.

At last Dennis released Janet and turned to Donna. "You look great, Donna." He gave her a friendly bear hug, then took each of them by an arm. "Let's dig your luggage out of the baggage belt."

On the drive to Aunt Flora's house, Dennis explained, "I've got the whole schedule worked out. Tonight, tomorrow, and tomorrow night, Janet's mother and aunt have you both. Monday, you're both coming to my house — and staying over."

"You're sure of this?" Janet asked dubiously.

"Then on Tuesday," Dennis said, ignoring the question, "I'll take you back to Coconut Grove so you can have the last two days there with your mother."

"How do you know it'll work out that way?" Janet asked. "My mother . . ."

"I've already checked it out with your mother and she thinks it's fine," Dennis said. "Any further suggestions, questions, or nervous remarks?" He leaned toward Janet and squeezed her hand. "Just leave everything to Uncle Dennis. He knows."

As the car wheeled along the sunlit strip of road, Donna felt extremely uneasy. Was it the forthcoming visit on Tuesday with Dennis's parents? Or was it something else? Her ESP was trying to tell her something, but she didn't have the faintest idea what it was.

Mrs. Bryson was overjoyed to see them. Aunt Flora's house was a simple five-room stucco bungalow, with a small flower garden in front and a glassed-in porch along the side.

"You two girls will be sleeping here," Janet's Aunt Flora announced, indicating two chintz-covered studio beds in a lovely plant-decorated room.

Since it was so late, Dennis soon said good-bye, leaving them to have a light snack — homemade cookies and fresh orange juice. Shortly after, the girls said good night to Mrs. Bryson and her sister and retired to the sunroom.

"Now what are you worrying about?" Donna was lowering the louvred shades as Janet started to undress. "Don't tell me it's Dennis's mother again."

"You get an A plus for that," Janet said. "Wait till you meet her. His father is okay, I guess."

"It doesn't matter how they are," Donna said reasonably. "Dennis and you are right for each other. That's all that matters."

"It isn't that simple, Donna. The Macfarlands aren't like us." Janet turned back the spread on her bed and slipped beneath the covers. "Dennis's mother can really give him a hard time, if she wants to." She sighed. "You'll see — on Tuesday."

The morning dawned bright and clear; the deep blue sky was crowded with translucent, fleecy clouds. As they drove along the slender strip of road connecting Coconut Grove and Miami Beach, Dennis raised the subject that was on their minds.

"What I don't like is the fact that those attacks are happening so much more often." He looked worriedly down at Janet sitting beside him.

133

"I agree," Donna said quietly, "but what can we do about it? Outside of coming down here for a visit, really, Dennis, we've been pushing through as fast as we can to find Janet's mother."

"You're sure it's all connected with your search?" Dennis asked.

"It's got to be that. Nothing else. The first strange man showed up right at the cemetery," Donna explained. "After that, everything started happening."

"Donna's positive everything started happening because of my father . . . because he died," Janet said.

"I wouldn't be so sure," Dennis said.

"Okay. What other explanation is there, Dennis?" Donna asked.

"I don't know." He looked puzzled. "But anything is possible."

Donna decided not to pursue the subject. The whole subject was too touchy, especially now, when Janet was about to meet Dennis's parents.

The Macfarlands lived in a beautiful, low-sprawling Spanish villa with an inner courtyard where terraced bedrooms with wrought-iron railings overlooked a splashing fountain.

As they went up the circular flagstone walk, a heavy dark mahogany door swung open and there stood Dennis's father and

134

mother. Mrs. Macfarland was a buxom woman with fringed false eyelashes and an artificial welcoming smile. Beside her, her small, dapper husband awaited them with a nervous smile.

"You're late, Dennis," his mother said.

Dennis consulted his wristwatch. "Only fifteen minutes, Mother. I'm sorry. Traffic was heavy."

"We're having Quiche Lorraine, and we were hungry, so I'm afraid we started lunch without you."

Dennis frowned. "Mother, really. What a way to meet someone. You know Janet — and this is her friend . . ."

He didn't have a chance to finish. Mrs. Macfarland cut in: "Now don't just stand in the doorway arguing, dear. Our lunch will get even colder." Then she said unsmilingly, "Hello, Janet. Of course we've met," and acknowledged Donna's presence with no change of expression as she led the way to the outside dining area beside the fountain.

The table was set beautifully on a terrace surrounded by poinsettia bushes. A water fountain splashed merrily on the back lawn, which ran all the way down to the edge of the bay. There a beautiful white cabin cruiser was docked.

Mr. Macfarland seemed very quiet and

unassuming, despite the fact that he owned a large boatyard, where Dennis had started to work after college to learn the business.

Lunch was uncomfortable. Mrs. Macfarland kept the conversation going largely by asking questions. Her favorite subject today was Janet. She asked a dozen personal questions of Janet and was anything but subtle. The climax came when she leaned forward just before dessert was served to say, "I understand you're an only child, Janet."

Since this was the third time she had mentioned Janet's background, Janet merely nodded. Why was Dennis's mother asking so many questions she already knew the answers to? Janet had met both of Dennis's parents last winter, right after she and Dennis had met at a rock concert on the beach. Dennis had met her parents, and she had met his. Now Mrs. Macfarland was running right through the same dialogue as last year. Something was definitely on her mind.

Donna had come to the same conclusion. Mrs. Macfarland clearly was bothered by something. It didn't seem to be the fact that Janet was from a middle-class working background. Nor did Mrs. Macfarland seem jealous of her son as some possessive mothers often were.

It could only be one thing. She had somehow learned that Janet was adopted.

A surge of anger rose inside Donna. What was the matter with people? Didn't they know adoptees were once just babies like everybody else? With one difference. Their unfortunate parents had had to give them up to strangers. In every other way there was no difference between an adopted child and the rest of the world. Couldn't Mrs. Macfarland see that?

Donna watched Janet as she tried to answer. "Yes, I'm an only child, Mrs. Macfarland."

"That's unusual," Mrs. Macfarland said. "Most people have two or three, at least."

"My parents didn't have any. That's why they adopted me." Janet said, her cheeks flushed and hot.

"Can we have the dessert now?" Mr. Macfarland asked, hoping to stem his wife's curiosity.

She ignored him and said to Janet, "Oh, that's right. I forgot."

"Mother, you know I told you," Dennis said, pushing back his chair. "Why don't I clear these dishes and get the cake plates?"

Incredibly, Mrs. Macfarland went right on. She smiled thinly at Janet. "Don't think me crude . . . or unkind," she said, "but Dennis is my child. My flesh and blood. A natural mother worries a great deal about her children. It's a matter of having enough information . . ."

"Mother!" Dennis said angrily.

Janet said, "Dennis, please." Then she turned to his mother. "I understand, Mrs. Macfarland. You don't know who I am, actually. But I was raised by two very good people who love . . . loved . . . me very much." She swallowed uncomfortably and went on. "That's about all I can say. I don't know who my real mother and father are. I'm hoping to find out one day . . . soon. When I do, I certainly hope they meet with your approval."

Good girl, thought Donna. That's telling her off. Under the table she stretched out a tentative toe and touched Janet's leg approvingly.

Mrs. Macfarland stiffened. "You may bring the chocolate cake in," she told the uniformed housekeeper.

"I wonder if we could take a swim after lunch?" Donna said brightly.

"Of course," Dennis's father said with a big smile. "Matter of fact, I want Dennis to take you young people out on the

Pleiades. It's spanking new and I've been dying to have him show her off."

"It sounds wonderful, Mr. Macfarland," Donna said. "Will we be able to go out very far?"

Dennis grinned at her. "Far enough for you to do some fancy water skiing," he said. "If you like, I mean."

"I like," Donna said. "Only I don't know how to water ski very well. Living in Philadelphia, I don't get to practice very often."

"Then this is your chance," Dennis said. "We aim to please."

The rest of the meal went by pleasantly, except for Mrs. Macfarland, who every now and then stole a meaningful look at her husband and her son. *I'll talk to you both later.* She might just as well have said it aloud.

As Dennis made conversation, sliced cake, and helped serve the coffee, Donna thought, It's okay now. We might just get through the rest of this visit without too much flak.

What she didn't know, what none of them could know, was what lay ahead of them, somewhere out there, in the clear blue waters of the bay.

* * *

139

Dennis took the helm of his boat and maneuvered it to where the water was a sleek, still pool of iridescent glass. There the three of them — Dennis, Janet, and Donna — took turns water skiing, diving, swimming, and lolling aboard deck, listening to Dennis's fabulous collection of cassettes, everything from rock to Bach to Elton John and Beverly Sills.

Then the sun began to drop toward the horizon. Its golden glow slowly deepened and layered the sky in dazzling shades of pink and red and purple. Donna, in for a last swim, reveled in the warm waters and the glorious air kicking her legs in a lazy half-float as she lay on her back looking up at the sky. She was not aware that she had drifted some twenty or thirty yards from the *Pleiades*. Perhaps two hundred yards away, a figure in a small boat was idly trolling. From where she was, it was hard to tell if it was a man, boy, or woman.

She rolled lazily over on her side, realized she was on the lee side of the boat, then turned over again and started to swim in a leisurely crawl back to the others.

That was when she saw it.

A shiny black streak coming toward her underneath the surface of the water. For

140

a long moment she watched and waited, her face just beneath the surface of the water, her legs doing a scissors kick to keep her afloat. What was it? All she saw was a large black form . . . a black thing moving speedily through the water. No mistake about where it was headed. Right at her.

She lifted her head from the water and screamed: "*Help! Help!*" again and again, as the water began to lap in small waves around her, over her shoulders, her head. The creature, the shark, the thing, whatever it was, came closer and closer. Furiously, she sped toward the boat, kicking her feet wildly to gain momentum, to agitate the waters and perhaps divert the dreadful black horror that was almost upon her. She turned her head back once as she rocketed through the water and saw it up close.

It was a man, a huge, black-clad figure, but a man.

Suddenly he was upon her, pulling her down. Water poured into her eyes, her nose. He was pressing her down hard, holding her shoulders, keeping her there. Her lungs swelled up, seared with fiery pain. She tried to hold her breath, to keep from ingesting water, but she couldn't last, she couldn't.

141

Help, she screamed silently under the water. Didn't they know, up above in the boat? Didn't they know what was happening to her?

She thrashed out, trying to free herself from the vise-like grip on her shoulders. Stars of pain exploded before her eyes, in her brain. *It's all over*, she thought. *I can't stand another second*. Her head was bursting, she couldn't breathe, she was going . . . going fast. All at once she was in a mind-out-of-body experience . . . she saw herself thrashing about on the sea floor. She was off a ways, watching the struggle, being no part of it. All she had to do was close her eyes and surrender, surrender to the warmth and peace of the water. But a light in her brain flashed *No!* and she was back in the stranger's grasp, his black-gloved hands were on her shoulders. She heard Pete's voice saying, "Use what you've got!" With a mightly effort she turned her head and bit down on the underside of the man's wrist. The black hand relaxed as her attacker doubled with pain, and Donna floated upward to the surface, where all was deathly still.

Chapter 10

The sky was black. The rows of houses were ghostly in the still of the night. She was walking down the street and she was afraid, deathly afraid. In any moment he might appear. He could run out from behind one of the dark alleys or come speeding down the road in a big black car that looked like a funeral hearse. She walked in terror. Her throat hurt, pains shot throughout her chest.

Then suddenly the street was ablaze. One of the houses was on fire. In a moment, the flames had skipped from building to building and the whole street was a giant inferno. She tried to cry for help, but couldn't. No sound came. Her legs wouldn't move; they were glued to the pavement.

Then she saw him. A tall, gentle-looking man with white hair and a kind smile. He was wearing a fireman's uniform and he was motioning to her to come to him. She yelled, "I see you! I'm trying to come to you!"

And then she woke up.

Her eyes blinked against the light in the room. Big pale-blue and yellow pansies danced on the wallpaper in an irregular pattern. Where was she?

"She's waking up," a voice said. "Thank God." It was a girl's voice, familiar.

"Donna? How do you feel?" A man's voice, but whose?

Then the two faces came closer. Janet's, pale pink, worried; and Dennis's, tan, lean, questioning.

A small sigh escaped her. Safe. She was safe.

"I'm okay," she said.

Janet bent down impulsively and kissed her. "Oh, Donna, Donna. You don't know what it's been like, waiting for you to come to. I thought I'd die." Janet squeezed Donna's hand gently as it lay on the yellow candlewick bedspread.

They decided there was no point in calling the police.

"It's the same situation as the time I was attacked at school," Janet said, shuddering, remembering.

144

"Right," Pete said. "No way to find him, with no way to identify him."

They turned their attention to Donna. It was much better than they had thought. They didn't even have to call a doctor. Donna felt weak, but that was all. Later, when she left the bed and was sitting in the sun parlor in one of the big wicker chairs with a light coverlet over her, it felt good to talk about it, to share the terror she had known in the murky waters beneath the *Pleiades*.

"We didn't hear you scream for help because you were on the opposite side from where we were on deck," Dennis explained.

"And the stereo was on," Janet said, "and . . ." She stopped suddenly and her cheeks flushed hotly.

And Donna knew. They had been kissing, Dennis and Janet, making out, and that's why it had taken them so long to realize something was wrong!

Dennis nodded. "Yeah. We were fooling around, Donna. Not a lot . . . nothing heavy." His jaw tightened. "Then I felt ripples coming out from both sides of the boat. You can't make that happen unless something is *underside* . . ."

Janet said, "At first we thought it was a big fish or something like that. Then I

145

couldn't see you anywhere, Donna." Her voice broke into a sob.

"Janet, don't," Donna said. "Everything's cool. I'm fine."

"I couldn't stand it if anything happened to you, Donna." Janet shuddered. "And I know now — after this . . . this thing today — I'm not letting you take any more chances. If there's more investigating to do, I'll do it on my own."

"That's ridiculous," Dennis said. "I won't let you."

"You don't have to worry about anything, Dennis. I just realized I'm scared too. I'm not going on with it." She dropped her head and looked away from them both. "I've had it! I'm not letting anyone get hurt. Not any more."

"You're just upset, Janet," Donna said quietly. "You don't really mean it, do you?"

"I'll never forget what you've done, Donna. But it's all over. I'm quitting. We're both quitting."

"Why? WHY?" Donna demanded.

Janet said firmly, "Because someone is out to harm me. To get me, ever since my father died. I don't know why. Maybe my father owed him something and didn't pay it and now he's going to get even."

"Do you know how foolish that sounds?" Donna said. "It can't be the reason."

"Right," Janet said. "I agree. We both know the real reason. Someone is trying to stop me from finding out who I really am. Well, whoever it is, he's won. Because we're not going on. Not you, not me."

"Janet's absolutely right," Dennis said. "You two have been taking too many risks." He addressed himself to Donna. "If your parents . . . if your parents knew what almost happened to you today . . ."

"I'm glad they're in Switzerland," Donna said soulfully. "I don't think they'd feel very good about it."

"Are you going to tell them?" Dennis said.

"Of course," Donna said. "When they come back. We try not to have secrets from each other. Oh, maybe some things we don't want the others to know, but never anything really important."

"Aha!" Janet leapt right in. "So you admit it! Today was serious. Donna, we're both stopping here. Right here."

"No," Donna answered stubbornly. "I won't agree. It means too much to you and your future." She bit her lip and glanced at Dennis.

He said, "If you're thinking about what

my mother said at lunch, please, don't take her too seriously. She says lots of things like that." He smiled ruefully. "She's just tactless, that's all." He stopped as neither girl spoke; he hadn't convinced them, that was plain. He cleared his throat and said deeply, sincerely, "I don't care who your real parents are, Janet. I know the mother and the father who raised you and that's good enough for me."

He took Janet's hand and held it, squeezed it. She turned her face toward him and they sat like that, quietly. Donna turned her head away and saw outside the windows the blue waters of the bay.

Something clicked and a picture flashed across her mind. Wind. Man. Father. Janet's father. White hair blowing in the wind, unreal. Something in a dream. What was he doing? It kept escaping her. Too hazy. She closed her eyes. She couldn't hang on to it at all.

"I love you," Dennis was speaking softly to Janet as Donna opened her eyes. "That's all that matters, isn't it?"

Janet said, "Yes," and stared down at her hands.

"You're no good at lying," Dennis said. "A three-year-old could do better."

"All right," Janet burst out. "I *do* want to know! I hate desperately the thought

148

of giving up! Hate it! I want to know who I really am, where I really came from, where my real mother is!" She brought her voice under control. "But I don't want to get Donna and me killed while we're trying to find out."

"Right," Dennis said fervently. "That's why I say, drop it now."

Janet said to Donna, sitting there with a faraway look on her face, "What are you thinking?"

Donna said, "I don't know. It's something I think I know — something that could help us maybe. I mean, to find your mother. But I can't pin it down. It keeps flashing into my head and out. I keep thinking it's important, it's something we need to know." She slammed a fist into her other hand. "It'll come back to me. It's got to!"

"Are you sure?" Dennis asked dubiously.

"It's bound to. It's just that I'm impatient," Donna explained. "Dr. Gordon says the best way to recapture a thought is to let go of all effort to remember it. Then it will float back naturally to your brain."

Dennis said unhappily, "What I wish is that you'd forget the whole thing. But I guess it's no use asking you?"

"It's up to Janet," Donna said, looking at her questioningly.

"What can I say?" Janet's voice was thick with feeling. "I do want to know. I do." She touched Dennis's arm. "You understand, don't you?"

He shrugged his shoulders and sighed. "I know when I'm licked. I won't talk any more about it, and I won't mention it to my parents when they come back for dinner. But . . ."

"But . . . ?" Donna asked warily.

"But I'm not letting either of you out of my sight until I put you on that plane back to Philadelphia," he warned. "And I'm going to tell Pete what happened down here, so he can arrange for . . ." He broke off lamely.

Donna said the rest for him: "You see? There's no way of knowing how or when they'll strike next. All we can do is try to stay out of dangerous situations as best we can, until we've got the information we need."

"I'm putting Pete on guard, though," Dennis said.

"Please don't," Donna begged. "Let us tell him ourselves, please. We're big girls now."

"Right," Janet said. "You have to let us handle it our way, Dennis."

So now the two young women were united in the effort. It made the rest of their stay at the Macfarlands much easier. Donna felt well physically. Her throat hurt very little and she was fit enough to handle anything. What bothered her was the elusive thing that flicked in and out of her mind, troubling her because she couldn't latch on to what it was. In the midst of conversation, she would suddenly drop out mentally and start probing. An indistinct, ghostly figure, trying to tell her something, show her something. Who was he? What was he trying to say?

Chapter 11

Their stay in Florida ended all too soon. The weather was flawless, which made it all the worse when they deplaned into the icy cold of Philadelphia, 10 degrees above zero.

Pete met them at the airport and hurried them out to the car and drove straight to Donna's home. Donna's sister Abbey had gone to stay with a friend in Virginia during the holidays.

They found the house dark but in perfect order. After they had started a fire and settled down with hot drinks before it, the girls brought Pete up to date. When he heard about the latest attack in Florida, he broke into their conversation angrily:

"I don't know what you think you're up to, Donna. So far you've both been lucky. Lucky, that's all. These people, whoever they are, are playing for keeps. Can't you see that?"

"Okay, I'll admit that it's getting more dangerous." She took a sip of the hot herb tea. "Of course, I don't think they meant to get *me* in Florida. I think it was Janet, don't you? I mean, we were wearing the same color bathing suits."

"What difference does it make? Neither of you is safe. What are you going to do about that?" His eyes narrowed. "Of course, I could always get in touch with your parents. I promised them I'd keep an eye on both of you while they were gone. I should think that might include letting them know what happened down in Florida."

"This is my responsibility, Pete, not yours." It was Donna's turn to be angry. "And not my parents', either. I'm an adult." Her tone lightened. "Furthermore, I like living. Really, Pete, that man in Florida got to me. I don't know when I've been so scared in my life. I promise that Janet and I will be super careful after this."

"You've said that before," he protested.

"Pete, we'll try to include you in anything we do from here on out. Will that satisfy you?" Donna asked.

That seemed to mollify Pete. He started asking questions and they went into more detail about their visit. Then Donna went into the kitchen to put the kettle on again. She moved about, taking crackers and cheese out, quartering some apples she found in the refrigerator.

From the living room, she could hear snatches of Janet and Pete's conversation.

". . . down to City Hall and went through the records . . ." Janet speaking.

". . . living there in 1940? It's a problem . . ." This from Pete.

". . . can't look all over the whole United States . . ." Janet again.

Then Pete's voice: ". . . should say not . . . nothing to go on . . ." Silence, then Pete again, ". . . your mother . . . grandfather . . . a fireman . . . moving away . . . out of state . . ."

Midway between refrigerator and kitchen table, Donna froze. Then she *knew*. In her excitement she dropped the plate of fruit she was holding. It crashed to the floor as she let out a cry.

Pete came charging into the kitchen, followed by Janet, anxiety on their faces.

"Donna! What happened?"

"Are you hurt? What is it?"

"I've got it! I've got it!" she yelled. She grabbed Pete around the neck and hugged and kissed him. Then she hugged Janet. All the while she yelled again and again, "I've got it!"

"Got what?" Pete demanded, pulling her to a halt.

"Oh, Pete, it's what you said in there to Janet." Donna put her arm around Janet's shoulder. "I don't know for sure if it will work out, but my ESP tells me it will! We'll make it work out!"

Janet looked squarely at Donna. "What will work out? All Pete and I talked about was where my mother's father and mother could be. I don't even know when they moved away from Baltimore, or where they moved to."

"Yes, but how about the things you *do* know?" Donna asked.

"You mean my grandfather's name?" Janet shrugged.

"Pete said your grandfather is . . . was . . . a fireman. That's a terrific clue," Donna said.

"Why?" Pete asked.

"Firemen and policemen work for the city," Donna explained. "What's more, they have pension plans, things like that." She turned to Janet. "If your grandparents moved away in 1952, let's say, it could have been because your grandfather retired or something. Firemen and policemen retire earlier than most people, because of the dangerous work they do."

Pete said, "You know, I think you're

right. If a man is a salesman in a shoe-
store in Pennsylvania and he moves to
California, you might as well give up. He
could get a job as a salesman in any business — coats, dishware, sports equipment..."

Janet broke in. ". . . or get a different
job, like driving a taxi, or doing car-
penter's or electrician's work . . ."

"Right," Donna said. "A fireman or a
policeman would usually stick to his own
line of work, and fire departments keep
special records and have a national organi-
zation, I imagine. And their pension plans
go on even if a fireman who's retired gets
a different job. So they have to keep mail-
ing his pension checks to wherever he is,
don't they?"

Pete shook his head and said, "Brains.
That's what you've got, baby."

Janet grabbed her, and with feeling
said, "We can go on now. Yes?"

"Yes. We're going right back to Baltimore, Janet — to pay a visit to the Fire
Department."

"When?" Pete asked.

"Tomorrow morning, early. The car is
sitting in the garage doing nothing."

"You can't go tomorrow. I've got the
kids from Jordan Center all day." He
paused, unhappily. "And Thursday I'm

156

working in registration with the faculty. I can't go with you until Friday."

Donna said, "Pete — I hope you're not asking..."

"Okay. I realize it's asking too much of you to wait until then, Donna." Resignedly, he added, "Just don't make the trip complicated. Go directly to the firehouse. Period. That's all." He looked directly at her. "Promise?"

For a long moment Donna said nothing, then, "Listen, Pete, we'll double-check everything beforehand for safety. No going down lonely alleys, or separating from each other even for a moment. Nothing like that. Okay?"

That seemed to please Pete. "It's okay, Donna. Just make sure you and Janet stick to those rules."

"What made you think of the fireman, Donna?" Janet asked.

"It was this nightmare I kept having after than man attacked me in Florida. I'd fall asleep and keep seeing this black figure. At first I thought it was the one who came after me and dragged me under the boat. Then I thought it was the man I saw at the cemetery in Washington the day of the funeral." Donna was reliving the moment as she was telling it. "When I heard you and Pete talking about 'fireman,' the whole dream flashed in my head and I saw it was your father, Janet, holding a fireman's hat."

"It's fantastic," Janet said. "You mean my father Bryson?"

"Yes," Donna said. "Now that I think of it, you were in the dream somewhere, but just for a moment." She hesitated. "Some day I'm going to ask Professor Gordon where these weird dreams of mine come from. And if she really believes in ESP, like I do."

"Great," Pete said. "But don't let your ESP run away with you. On this trip to Baltimore, keep it simple. Don't take any chances. If you need help, call me, understand?"

The car tooled merrily along the thruway, heading for Baltimore. Beside Donna, Janet was quiet. What was she brooding about?

"I wonder where my mother is living now?" Janet said, as Donna guided the car toward the exit lane. Then Janet sighed and pursed her lips together. "*If* she's living," she said softly.

Donna said nothing, only thought how terrible it was not to know where your flesh and blood mother was, or even if she were alive or dead.

"What will we do when we get to Baltimore? Have you thought about it?" Janet sounded uncertain. "I can't just walk into a firehouse and tell them I'm Albert Willins' illegitimate granddaughter, can I?"

"No. Of course not. As soon as they know the real reason, they'll clam up, like everybody else, like all the people who think it's wrong to stir up trouble, or whatever they keep telling us."

"Why would they give out the kind of information we need?" Janet persisted. "Why should they tell us, strangers, where my grandparents moved to?"

"We'll deal with that when we come to it." Donna tapped her forehead with a knowing finger. "Leave it to 'The Brain,' baby. I've got whole parts of it that haven't even been used yet."

"You can say that again," Janet said, and they laughed, easing the atmosphere.

At the corner of a broad street where a policeman was directing traffic, Donna pulled up and rolled down the window.

"I wonder if you could tell us where the nearest firehouse is?" she asked.

"Why?" The handsome young cop eyed the two girls approvingly. "You planning to have a fire?"

"Only in the fireplace." Donna grinned. "Listen, officer, is there a central firehouse in Baltimore? Or are they all just branches or something?"

"That's a good question. There is a main fire department — headquarters and all — on Vesey Street."

He gave them directions and said, "I wouldn't mind buying you two a couple of beers sometime. Like, tonight. I go off duty at 6:00."

"That's great," Donna said. "You just come to Philadelphia at say, 6:30 tonight. That's where we'll be — we live there."

"Are you serious? Philadelphia?" He was crestfallen.

"Yes," both Donna and Janet answered.

"It's always that way," he said mournfully. "The winners either don't like me or they live in Philadelphia or China or someplace. Actually," he said, "I guess my wife and kids wouldn't like it anyway."

"Cheer up," Donna said. "It's the same with us. All the winners are either in Baltimore or Alaska or someplace. Or they're married."

Suddenly it was very funny to the three of them. Passing traffic and pedestrians on the clear, white, cold street of Baltimore stared. The policeman tapped a badge on his jacket that read 'William Migliore,

No. 8473.' "If you ever need me, just holler."

"We will," they said delightedly. "Thanks."

At Vesey Street, the firehouse, with its red and white painted front, gleamed in the noontime sun. Inside, the firemen greeted them with wolf whistles from a table around which they were seated playing cards. The table was crowded with soggy containers of coffee and the remnants of sandwiches.

Donna and Janet approached a stocky young man seated near the door of a glass partitioned booth, at the head of the card-players' table.

The stocky fireman rose from his armchair. "Excuse us, please," he said. "We've been on duty since 2:00 A.M. and we've had four false alarms, and two legitimate calls. We're just trying to keep awake until quitting time."

"You don't have to apologize to us," Donna said. "We're here to get some information."

Instantly, the fireman cooled. "What do you want to know?"

"It's for my friend here," Donna said. "Her mother was on the outs with the family for a while. Now Janet wants to

161

track down her cousin. Ohhh, I almost forgot. Her uncle was a fireman."

The fireman said to Janet, "I see. What's your uncle's name?"

Donna interposed quickly, "Willins. Albert Willins. Her cousin is a lot older than Janet, but they were very close."

"I'll see what I can get hold of," the burly fireman said. "You ladies wait here." He turned to the other firemen. "You guys better clear out and get the upstairs quarters policed up."

One young fireman who had been eyeing Janet said to the other two, "Okay, you guys go upstairs. I'll take care of this."

The other two older men looked at him knowingly and left.

"So your uncle was a fireman?" he said to Janet.

"Yes," she said. "Right here in Baltimore."

"That makes him A-okay in my book," the young fireman said. "His niece, too. What did you say your name was?"

Janet swallowed. "Janet Willins."

At that moment the burly fireman returned with a thick book in his hands. He motioned them over to the desk to look at the book with him. There they found the names of Janet's grandparents and family. "Willins, Albert. Wife Teresa, son Richard, daughter Ellen." Janet's mother!

The burly fireman was looking at them, curiously. His eyes were suspicious as he watched them and waited for them to speak.

Donna said, "Oh, your cousin Richard!" giving Janet the clue. "You used to be so crazy about him when you were kids. Isn't that right, Janet? Isn't he the one you always told me about?"

Janet picked up the cue. "Absolutely," she said. "He was such a tease. I wonder where he's living now."

The burly fireman shook his head firmly. "We can't give you that information. Anything in the directory, well, that's different. Public information. But we don't hand out any other details about our men."

The young fireman said to Janet, "How did you know your uncle doesn't work here anymore?"

Before Janet could answer, the telephone rang. The burly man picked up the phone and started a conversation with someone. The young fireman motioned the girls outside. There he said, "How did you know that your uncle moved away?"

Janet said, "Oh, I heard it from the

family someplace. I think it was my cousin Jeffrey." Suddenly she was inventing a whole new tribe of cousins and uncles.

"The chief will kill me for doing this, but I think your uncle is retired. I think he moved to someplace out West. I could look it up for you." He added slyly, "If you gave me your phone number, maybe we could meet. I could call you, or something."

His meaning was all too clear. He had been ogling Janet from the first moment they came into the firehouse. Now, true to her style, Janet demurred. "Oh, I'm afraid that would be im—"

"Give us *your* home number," Donna said quickly, noticing that inside his office, the chief was impatiently ending his phone call with whomever it was. "We, I mean she, she'd be glad to meet you some evening, wouldn't you, Janet?" She nudged Janet with her elbow.

"Oh, yes, I'd be glad to. What's your phone number?"

"WALNUT 3-7488. Kresky, Paul, is my name. I'm single," he said meaningfully. "How about tonight?"

"I think that would be all right."

Now he was very anxious to please. "That's not all," he said. "There's something else that would be a lot more important. I could tell you . . ."

He broke off suddenly as the chief stepped outside the door of the glass booth and yelled, "Kresky, come here! I want to talk to you!"

The young fireman obeyed instantly. Whatever he was about to tell them, it was gone now. The chief motioned Kresky into his glass booth and stepped outside, approaching the girls.

"I'm sorry. You ladies have to go now. We can't give you any personal information. That's final."

Donna and Janet thanked him and left, throwing a final friendly glance back in Fireman Kresky's direction. If he noticed it, he gave no sign. The chief was obviously bawling him out.

"What do you say now?" Donna asked as they headed for the car. "Have we got a lead or have we got a lead?"

"We have," Janet said. "The problem is, maybe we got him in trouble. Maybe we shouldn't call him."

"We're not going to phone him at the firehouse. We'll call him at five o'clock at his house."

"Why five o'clock?"

"I noticed his hours on the time schedule posted on the wall. It said, 'Kresky — 8:00 A.M. to 4:00 P.M.'"

"The chief was sure letting him have it,"

Janet said worriedly. "Maybe he's afraid to take any chances now. Maybe he won't want to see us again."

"Do me a favor, will you? Stop being such a Calamity Jane. The man is madly in love with you, couldn't you tell?"

"He probably falls madly in love five times a week. He's that type. Yeccch."

"I think he is. But we can't let that stop us from taking advantage of it."

Janet consulted her wristwatch. "We have about an hour and a half to wait. I'm hungry. Let's go someplace for some tea and a nice slab of layer cake."

"You're hopeless," Donna said. But she let Janet lead the way to a coffee shop a few doors away. It seemed to be largely inhabited by lawyers and people who worked for the city, judging by the conversation around them. They took seats in a small, lamplit booth and gave their orders.

As they waited for their food, Janet said, "Donna, I'm all confused. Why in the world did you say Albert Willins was my uncle when he's really my grandfather? I don't get it."

"It happened as I was making up that story about your mother being on the outs with her family," Donna explained. "It suddenly dawned on me that they might not like the idea of a woman not speaking to her own *father*. I thought anyone could understand a sister and brother having a disagreement and not speaking for a while. But a *father* — especially a father who's a fireman? I thought they might get angry enough to refuse to give us any information."

"You're absolutely right," Janet agreed. "But it made me nervous, honestly."

"Me too. But it worked out — at least so far it has." Donna threw her long brown hair back impatiently. "What I'm hoping for now is that we get an answer to whose license plate was on that car last month."

"Why should it take so long?" Janet asked.

"Because some numbers and a letter are missing. That means they have to rely on mathematical probabilities — which increases enormously the amount of cars with similar license plates."

"What do you mean by mathematical probabilities? I never could figure them out." As an art major, Janet was very weak in mathematics.

"It means how the odds increase when you're dealing with multiple progressions," Donna said.

"That's a big help," Janet said.

"I'll simplify it. Take the example where you have a piggy bank and you decide to save pennies."

"Are you kidding?"

"No. Say you start with one penny, and double the amount every day. First day, one penny. Second day, two pennies. Third day, four pennies."

Janet said, "Got that."

"Good. Fourth day, eight pennies . . ."

"Fifth day, sixteen pennies. And the day after that, thirty-two pennies, and the day after that sixty-four pennies. Right, teacher?"

"Right. On the seventh day you've got sixty-four pennies in your piggy bank."

"So what? That's no big deal."

"It isn't? Listen, Einstein — if you keep doubling the amount every day for one month, or thirty days, how much will you have?" Donna asked.

Figuring rapidly, Janet made a guess. "Eight hundred dollars? No, wait, something like eight thousand dollars?"

"Something like — over a million dollars," Donna answered.

"Really? A million?" Janet whistled. "Just from doubling one miserable penny?"

"It's actually $1,684,322," Donna said. "That gives you an idea of how mathematical progression works. Multiples increase the chances high into the thousands and millions, especially if you're dealing with combinations of numbers and letters in as big an amount as those on a license plate."

"Sometimes I wonder how we ever got to be such good friends," Janet said. "I hate the subjects you're so good at."

"You know I can't draw a straight line," Donna said. "How much time do we have to kill before we make that call?"

"Less than half an hour," Janet said.

"Let's pay our check and walk around until then."

As they waited for the waitress to write out the check, Janet's face resumed her familiar worried expression.

"You worrying again, Jan?" Donna asked.

"I can't help it, Donna. I really can't. If Paul Kresky gives us my grandfather's address, it means I'll be seeing . . . my mother soon. I get scared thinking about what will happen then," Janet said miserably.

"Janet, you're not chickening out again, are you?" Donna said.

"No," she said firmly. "I've got to find my mother, no matter how awful it may turn out."

"Good girl. You're in this to the end, right?"

"To the end, Donna." Janet sighed heavily. "To the bitter end, whatever it may bring."

Outside, they walked in the cold winter air until it was time to call. As Janet stepped into a phone booth, Donna said, "Be friendly, Janet. He can really help us."

"Don't worry," Janet said, and dialed. Then Donna heard, "Hello . . . yes, it's Janet Willins. No, of course I didn't forget you, Paul. How could I?" Here she gave a girlish giggle, then, "Sure, we can meet you . . . I'm with Donna, remember? . . . No, I can't leave her any place . . . I'm sorry. . . . When? Six o'clock . . . Where? . . . The Golden Calf, Highway 724 . . . Oh, I can't wait to see you either, Paul."

When she hung up, she said, "Ugh, I feel like such a fake. He thinks I have a crush on him. But he says he's got some really important information for me."

"Let's get right over there," Donna said enthusiastically. "On the way, you can tell me what he said."

"He mentioned something about Vermont . . . something about my grandfather living up there in some out-of-the-way place. If that's so . . ." her voice trailed off. Then she straightened up in her seat and said, "Wherever he lives, I'll find him. I'll find a way to get there."

"That's the spirit," Donna said warmly. "We're hot on the trail now." Donna could hardly keep the pleasure out of her voice. Moment by moment, Janet seemed to be gathering strength. Above all, what they needed now was a direct clue to Janet's family.

Paul Kresky came through with that clue. When they pulled into the driveway next to the Golden Calf, he was waiting for them. He got out of his cream-colored sports car and hurried over to them.

"Hi, baby! Great to see you again."

People in neighboring cars turned around to look as he bent down and kissed Janet like a long lost friend.

"Why don't you get in?" Donna said sweetly to him as he stood beside the open door beside Janet's seat in front. Without waiting for an answer, she reached over and unlocked the back door. "Sit back here so we can both look at you."

He got into the back of the car and tapped Janet on the shoulder so roughly she had to keep from wincing. "You didn't think I would let you down, did you, baby?" he said.

"Of course I didn't." Janet made it

sound warm and enthusiastic. "I know it wasn't easy to find out stuff about someone who hasn't been with your Fire Department in fifteen years," she said admiringly.

"I've been around, and I know how to handle myself," he said. "I guess it's hard for you ladies to understand how these things work. What happened was, I remembered that a letter came in a few months ago about your uncle, Albert Willins, asking about his pension check. You know he retired a few years ago and it seems his check got fouled up somehow, so he asked us to investigate."

Donna and Janet were elated, although neither one said anything. Was it possible he had the actual address of Albert Willins?

"I don't have your uncle's address. What I did get was your cousin Richard's address. He's a fireman, too, and he's the one who wrote in about his father's pension check."

It was dark in the car, but from the light of the restaurant coming in through the window, she read, "Richard Willins, Fireman First Class, 201 Talbot Avenue, Brooklyn, New York."

"This is wonderful, Paul," Janet said,

with real enthusiasm this time. "How can I ever thank you?"

"Well, for starters, I was hoping maybe we could go out tonight." He glanced in Donna's direction, then added, "Alone."

"That's impossible," Janet said. "We have to get back to Philly right away. And it's starting to snow, as you can see . . ."

He frowned in disappointment and said, "Gee. I thought you were staying in town for a couple of days."

Janet shook her head. "We have to get right back. I'm sorry."

"When are you coming down here again?" he asked sulkily.

"I don't think I will be back," Janet said.

"How about giving me your address in Philly?" he persisted. "I could run up there and see you on a weekend."

"Oh, they wouldn't like that at school." Janet shook her head. "They're very strict about that."

"School? You mean you're still a school kid? Boy, I sure had you figured wrong."

Donna said quickly, "That's the way it goes, Paul. You can't win them all." She turned the car keys and started the motor. "We've really got to move. But we do appreciate what you've done."

"Oh, sure," he said sarcastically. He got out of the car and slammed the door.

173

"Wow, he's angry," Janet said as they sped off. "I feel terrible, the way we treated him."

"I can't see why," Donna said. "Men who play that flirting game have got to expect rejection sometimes. You know he only did you that favor because he thought he could get something going with you. And I mean something heavy."

"Right. I felt it too," Janet said.

Donna concentrated on driving on the ride back. Janet stared at the snowflakes settling on the windshield, cozy in the warm car. Yet both, deep underneath, had in mind one thought: When and where would the attacker strike next? Since they'd gotten back from Florida last week, there'd been nothing. Was it the calm before the storm? A sign that he was ready to move in on them again?

And now they were close to the end of the trail. Donna sighed as she realized her parents would be back on Saturday. Five days. They couldn't wait that long. Paul Kresky might get the wind up and call Janet's uncle to tell him about their visit. Anything to mess up their plans . . . he'd seemed angry enough when he left them. Saturday . . . No, it wouldn't wait. They had better get into action right away.

Chapter 12

Because they had promised to check everything out with him, Donna and Janet met Pete later that night in Benson's Ice Cream Parlor. Pete said, "I'm ordering the Benson Five Dollar Super Sonic Sundae and three spoons. You two look like you need it, so I'll break training to keep you company."

Donna giggled. "How unselfish of you, Pete." She paused. "You've been wonderful. If there's ever anything we can do to thank you..."

Pete half shut his eyes and leered at them. "Sure thing. I was hoping maybe we could get together one night. I mean, alone." He winked at Donna, then at Janet. "I mean, alone with the two of you. How about it?"

He sounded so much like Fireman Kresky, it broke the girls up. He asked what they were laughing at, and they told him about Paul Kresky and what he'd told them.

Pete was impressed. "You mean you know where your Uncle Richard lives?" Janet nodded happily. "You're getting there, you two. When I think that you really started out of nowhere, I've got to hand it to you. You're operating like big-time private eyes."

Donna said, "It's all seemed like such a wild goose chase so many times . . . it's exciting to know we're almost there."

"Where's there?" Pete said. "You'd better include me in, you know. Wherever *there* is!"

"I mean the whole bit, Pete. Finding out exactly where Janet's mother is, getting them together . . . face to face."

Janet said softly, "You know, I still can't believe it. That we're so near to the end of the trail."

"I don't know how we're going to handle it," Donna said, frowning. As Pete and Janet looked at her curiously, she added, "We can't let your Uncle Richard know the real reason we want to contact his sister — your mother. At least not at first. He could put a stop to everything right there."

"Then how can we do it?" A note of despair crept into Janet's voice.

Donna threw her a warning look and said, "We'll think of something. There're three good brains sitting here. We're bound to come up with something."

"Yeah," Pete said. "How about calling up and pretending you're doing some kind of market research — you know, 'How many members are there in your family,' etc. etc.?"

"It might not work, Pete," Donna said. "And if it doesn't, we'll have trouble trying to approach him again."

Janet, who had been sitting thoughtfully, said, "Why can't we do something like we did at the firehouse?"

"What was that?" Pete asked.

"I told them we wanted to find out where my grandfather lived because my mother and her brother weren't friends any more and I wanted to track down my cousin," Janet said. "The daughter of my Uncle Richard."

"Hey, take it easy. Cousins, aunts, uncles — I can't keep them straight," Pete said drily. "It's getting too complicated."

Donna cut in with a small squeal. "Pete! Wait! Janet's got it!"

"I have?" Janet asked. "What have I got?"

"The approach. How to contact Richard

Willins by phone." She studied the problem a moment. "We have to get someone to call him — a woman of thirty-eight or forty. She has to say she's a girlfriend from high school of his sister Ellen Willins." She stopped and looked at Janet. "Your mother." Then, she went on slowly, "This woman should say that Ellen Willins moved away with her family in 1958 and she's dying to know what happened to her. What do you think of that?"

Pete said, "I think it's great. There's just one little problem." Donna and Janet stared at him. "How did you get his address?"

"That's easy," Donna said. "The woman can say she was visiting in New York and saw his name in the phone book, and just took a chance he was the same Richard Willins."

Pete shook his head in mock disgust. "Boy, you sure are getting to be terrific at making up instant lies."

"Think nothing of it," Donna said. It was her turn to leer at Pete. "It's the way we big-time private eyes operate."

Janet said, "The only thing is, we need a woman of forty. Who can we get to make the phone call?"

Donna said, "Who else? The family actress . . ."

"Abbey!" they shrieked and started laughing.

"When are we going to do this?" Janet said, getting excited now.

"Tonight," Donna said. "We can't waste any time."

"I'll drive you to the house," Pete said.

At that moment the waitress bore down on them with a huge oval platter loaded with balls of multi-colored, multi-flavored ice cream, doused in chocolate syrup, strawberry sauce, layered with bananas and nuts and pineapple, the whole outrageous assortment topped with a small mountain of fresh whipped cream. They all groaned with mock shame and genuine pleasure and dove in.

"We'll make up for this tomorrow by going on the diet of the world," Janet promised, as she conveyed a spoonful of the gooey sundae toward her mouth.

"You never make up for a spree like this," Pete cautioned. "Thousands of carbohydrates — terrible for the skin, the stomach . . ." — this, with his spoon already dug into a giant portion.

"You said a mouthful," Donna said, interrupting Pete. "No making up for this disaster."

"Speaking of mouthfuls, I notice you're doing your bit," Pete said.

"Just trying to speed you two up," Donna teased. "We have work to do at my house."

A half hour later, at the house, they were shocked by Abbey's appearance when she opened the door. Her face was greenish gray, accentuated by dark-brown and purple circles under her eyes.

"You should have told me you were bringing Pete!" she shrieked accusingly at Donna. In her confusion, she had lapsed from her British accent, and sounded just like what she was, an insecure teenager hurled into an embarrassing situation and unable to handle it. After she let them inside and explained that the paste on her face was a youth mask, designed to remove wrinkles and crow's feet around her eyes, she retreated to her room and returned wearing a long white flowing negligee with yellow boa cuffs and hem, the latter sweeping the floor like a train.

"Mother will kill you," Donna said, "when she finds out you've borrowed her gift from Dad."

"The only way she can find out is if you tell her," Abbey pouted.

"I won't, unless she asks me," Donna said. "Abbey, I wonder if you could do an enormous favor for Janet."

"What is it?" Abbey said suspiciously.

After they told her, Abbey was delighted to oblige. She looked off dreamy-eyed for a moment, then an older, more sedate tone of voice emerged from her lips. The others pronounced it perfect.

"You sound exactly like Mrs. Fayne next door," Donna said.

"That's who I was imitating," Abbey explained. She really was a gifted mimic.

Ten minutes later, the long-distance operator had put the call through. Following the instructions Donna had given her and sounding very adult, Abbey said when Richard Willins came on the line:

"Yes, my name is Mrs. Wright. But back in high school with Ellen, I was Bibi Hart. I don't know if you remember me . . . that's right, I was three years behind you, just like your sister Ellen . . . what? . . . I just wanted to get in touch with her . . . we used to be such good friends, I was wondering where she's living now so I could write to her . . . sure, I'll wait . . ."

They held their breaths as they stood in a small circle around Abbey, wondering, waiting. She said in a hoarse whisper, "Sssh. He told me to hang on . . . I don't know why." It was ages, it seemed, before she evidently heard the voice again, and she said, "Yes, I'm here. What's that?

181

Requena? I see . . ." She began to write furiously on the pad beside the telephone. "Oh, Vermont? I see . . . I'm so happy for her . . . What's that? . . . Yes, I have two children also. Yes, we *were* so much alike . . . I think I have all the information I need. Really, I don't know how to thank you." Now, she was beginning to get carried away. Always the ham, Abbey began to elaborate, "You sound so interesting, Mr. Willins. Perhaps we could meet some time, when my husband and the children . . ." She yelped as Donna kicked her on the shin.

"That's enough, you idiot!" Donna hissed. "You'll ruin everything!"

Abbey came to her senses, sedately thanked the man at the other end, and hung up.

With a long, purple-tinted fingernail, she indicated the piece of paper she had been writing on. "Look at that," she said triumphantly. "Everything you wanted to know but were afraid to ask."

"Thank you, Bette Davis," Donna said. "The way you were carrying on over the phone, I expected you to burst into tears and fling yourself on the mercy of the court at any moment."

Abbey said, darkly, "Don't think I couldn't have done it, either. I had him eating out of my hand. Really," she said, batting her mascaraed eyelashes at Pete, "I don't know why, but men are so much easier for me to deal with than women." She looked sharply at Donna. "Even my own sister."

Her own sister was studying the information on the sheet.

"Listen, Janet, it's all here. Abbey did a good job. See? Your mother married a man named Michael Requena. She's living up in Vermont and has two children, a boy and a girl."

Janet took the paper, trembling. "A boy and a girl — they're my half-brother and half-sister. And this is where my mother really lives." She sat down suddenly on the sofa. "My knees are shaky."

"We know how you must feel, Janet," Donna said, taking her hand. "It's a big shock for anyone." Donna looked appealingly at Pete.

"Want to go home?" Pete asked Janet.

"I do," Janet told him. "I need time to think about everything."

A few minutes later when the two young women were home and undressed, ready for bed, Janet said, "What bothers me, Donna, is that my mother probably never told her husband about me. Then what?"

"It's perfectly possible she didn't —

especially since she wasn't married to your father," Donna said. "Still, there must be a way . . ."

Janet rubbed a weary hand across her forehead. "I swear, it's too much for me to think about now. I'm frightened to death at just the thought of seeing my mother." She sighed. "Anyway, how do we arrange to meet her?"

"I don't know," Donna admitted. "Maybe we should go right up to New York, where you could meet your Uncle Richard in person. Of course you would first have to tell him the truth about why you were there." She paused. "Then, if it was okay with him, he could talk to your mother secretly, so she wouldn't have to tell her husband about you if she didn't want to."

Janet brightened. "That's right! We could do it that way! If you came with me, I'd be willing to meet him and tell him how I feel about wanting to see my mother." Her chin firmed. "After all, he's my blood relative, too. My uncle. His mother and father are my grandparents! But that's not all. What I want is to . . ." her voice quavered, "all I want is to see my mother."

"Then it's settled," Donna said, going to Janet and patting her shoulder affectionately. "How would you like to take off tomorrow morning for New York?"

"I can't," Janet said. "I've got that bio exam to make up, remember?"

"Right," Donna said with disappointment. "And we have to phone first, I guess, to be sure of meeting your uncle. Oh well, I guess we can afford one day. But I wish I had something constructive to do to fill in the time tomorrow."

At that moment, the phone rang.

Chapter 13

It was John Harbaugh, Mr. Rockford's law clerk.

"Excuse me for calling at this hour. I thought you'd be in by now — I've been trying to get you all evening," he explained. "It's about that license number. I got a phone call from the Motor Vehicle Bureau down in Baltimore. They've located the owner of the car."

Donna said, "Oh, John, who is it? It means so much to us — especially right now."

"Keep cool, Donna. The man's name is Thomas Johnson. He lives right here in Philadelphia."

Donna exploded with excitement. "Johnson? I knew it!"

"Knew what?"

"Never mind. Did you get his address?"

"Did I get it? Are you kidding? Do you know who Thomas Johnson is?" John sounded amazed. "Listen, sweetie, the guy is a big shot. A real biggie. Head of the City Planning Board. Senior Representative in the State Legislature."

"He is?" Donna asked, unbelievingly. "Are you sure?"

"I'm positive. Your father has met him on various occasions. City Council meetings, things like that."

"I can't believe it," Donna said. "Still, there may be a reason for it . . ."

"Do you mind telling me what you're up to?" John Harbaugh asked.

"I'm sorry, John. Truly I am. I wish I could tell you . . . but I'm not sure of anything myself just now."

"You know, you better just hold things till your dad gets back on Sunday. That's what I think."

"I'm sorry, John," Donna said hurriedly, "we have to go now." She hung up as he was still issuing warnings into the phone.

"What was that all about?" Janet asked.

"I'm not sure." Donna looked earnestly at Janet. "Do you know who that car belongs to — the one that came at us that day down in Baltimore?"

Janet shook her head. "No."

When Donna told her, Janet said with disbelief, "Why would a man like that be interested in either of us?"

Donna got up and walked over to the small kitchenette. "I can't imagine. How about a cup of herb tea? I think we need a conference."

"I'd love it." Janet sat up in bed and tucked the covers cozily about her. "How about a couple of cookies with it?"

"Not on your life," Donna said. "Every time you get nervous you want to eat — and it's always something sweet. Don't forget that Banana Boat." She grimaced. "How about an apple and a piece of cheese?"

Janet shrugged. "I can't win with you. Okay."

When Donna brought the tea tray over, she said, "It's possible, you know, that someone borrowed Mr. Johnson's car and used it without his knowledge."

"That's right," Janet agreed. "Whoever is out to get us may have asked to use the car as a favor. He could be anyone."

Donna considered that, then shook her head again. "It could be — but somehow I don't feel it is. Also — it's not someone who's out to get 'us.' The motivation centers around *you*." Donna's brow wrinkled in thought.

"Now what are you thinking, Sherlock?" Janet demanded.

"Something just flashed into my head,

Jan. You remember that day we first went to The Perry Home? And met Mrs. Fitch?"

"How could I forget?" Janet said dourly. "What a beast."

Donna snapped her fingers. "I know! I remember now! Of course, that's what it was!" She grinned with pleasure.

"I'm glad you're so happy," Janet said with annoyance.

"I'm sorry. It's just that I think pieces of the puzzle are beginning to fall into place." Donna sat down on the bed next to Janet. "That first day, when Mrs. Fitch went out of the office, I saw this note on your folder. Something with the name 'Johnson' on it. 'Mr. Johnson.' I don't remember the first name." Donna jumped up so quickly Janet's tea spilled over into the saucer. "I've got it!" She ran across the room and rummaged in a stack of papers and magazines on top of a low bookcase.

Finally she said, pulling out a pale yellow pamphlet, "Just wait a minute!" She riffled through the pages of the little booklet and then yelled triumphantly, "Thomas Johnson, Trustee and Chairman of the Board."

"Chairman of what board?"

Donna slapped the open page of the pamphlet and shoved it at Janet, who

189

looked at it for a moment and then whistled softly. "Whew — that's a coincidence, isn't it?"

"Coincidence?" Donna said, incredulously. "Can't be. Someone's trying to hurt you, Janet — ever since your father died. Then someone tries to run you down with an automobile we were lucky enough to get the number of. And the car belongs to Mr. Thomas Johnson. And guess who he is? A major trustee of the orphan home you came from — The Perry Home!" She sat down shaking her head. "Uh-uh. No coincidence, Janet. I can't buy that."

"Okay. Then suppose you're right. Suppose he's behind the whole thing — why in the world would he want me hurt, or dead?" Janet said in bewilderment.

"I don't know. There's got to be a reason, though. I'm going to find out what it is."

"How can you? It can't be done."

"I don't know. But I'll think of something. You'll see."

"Can't I help?"

"You've got your bio exam to make up, remember?"

Janet sighed. "Right. I'm going to set the alarm for two o'clock and get up to study for it. You'd better get some sleep."

But when Donna got into bed, sleep

eluded her for a long time. Tomorrow was when she would have to handle it. It wouldn't be easy, but she began to develop a scheme that might help her invade the sanctuary of Mr. Thomas Johnson.

Promptly at 9 o'clock the next morning, Donna opened the glass doors of the offices of "Thomas Johnson, Counselor-at-Law, State's Attorney," and entered the plush red-carpeted anteroom. A slender, sleek-haired receptionist dressed in high fashion surveyed Donna's casual jeans and jacket outfit with disapproval.

"I'm sorry. Mr. Johnson isn't in. I suggest you come back in an hour or two. Although," she added dubiously, "I doubt very much if he will see you without your explaining to me first why you want to see him."

"I'll take my chances," Donna said coolly. "If you don't mind, I'll just sit here and wait." From where she stood, she could look through the glass partition to see the entrance to Mr. Johnson's private office.

The receptionist obviously did mind, but could do nothing about it. She went back to her typing, which gave Donna an opportunity to take a good look around. Directly in front of her on the handsomely paneled

wall was a large oil painting in a heavy
gold frame. The man in the painting looked
cold, austere, almost cruel. Donna frowned.
There was something about the mouth,
the chin that held her attention. She had
seen this man before, somewhere. How
ridiculous. The man in the painting was
not young . . . perhaps in his sixties. The
clothes he was wearing were not modern.
Donna remembered seeing pictures of her
grandmother and grandfather taken years
before . . . in the 1940's or 50's. The
clothes her grandfather wore then were
like those the man in the painting had on.
There was a small metal plaque at the
base of the painting that said, "Thomas
Johnson I," then under it, the artist's
name, "Sewell," and the date "1957."

She looked at the glass door leading to
Mr. Johnson's office — it was half ajar,
and she saw "Thomas Johnson — Private." Was the man in the painting related
to the man she was waiting to see? Why
did he look familiar to her? Where could
she possibly have seen him?

As she was pondering this, the telephone
rang and she heard the receptionist say,
"Yes, I have it someplace in the files. I'll
look it up and call you back."

She came to the window of the glassed-
in office, looked anxiously into the recep-

tion room, saw that Donna was still there; she shook her head disapprovingly and disappeared through a doorway beyond the small office.

It was an opportunity Donna couldn't resist. She leapt to her feet and hurried to the open door of Thomas Johnson's office. Inside was a huge mahogany desk, a sofa, some comfortable sidechairs. On a table behind his desk there was an array of photographs; she stepped through the doorway tentatively. She wanted so much to learn about Mr. Thomas Johnson, she decided to take the risk.

Quickly she crossed the room and went right to his desk. Piles of papers were neatly aligned on it; one pile was weighted down with a thick book atop it, engraved in gold, "Thomas W. Johnson, II," then in smaller type on it, "Daily Diary." She flicked the pages of the diary open . . . going back to October and November. On a page she spotted an entry with the lone word "Fitch" and the time, "2:30 P.M." At the sound of a door closing outside, she slammed the diary shut and looked up anxiously and waited. Nothing. No further noise, no one in sight. She turned around to look at the group of photographs on the table behind the desk, over at the window. There were several photographs of varying sizes, obviously taken at different times. There was a picture of a handsome man and a slim, blond woman beside him, in their twenties or thirties. A small boy was holding the man's hand. Next to that portrait was one of a handsome young man about twenty years old. Donna felt a small excited shock of recognition. He was much younger, his hair was differently styled, but there was a resemblance to the stern-faced man in the painting out in the reception room, Thomas Johnson II. His clothes and haircut were similar to those of the older man.

She stood there a long moment, lost in thought.

"Would you mind telling me what you are looking for?" The voice was harsh, demanding.

She jumped in surprise, then her face crimsoned with guilt. There in the doorway, glowering at her, stood a tall, imposing man, impeccably dressed, eyes narrowed. His bearing notified the onlooker that here was a Very Important Person. He was gray-haired and obviously in his early or mid-fifties.

Donna was momentarily paralyzed. She could think of nothing to say to him. For a long moment they stood like that, in silence; then she recovered and pointed to the picture of the young boy in the snap-shot. She said, "Oh, excuse me. I saw this photograph from across the room — I was waiting out there for Mr. Johnson." She hesitated, knowing she was sounding like a slow-witted ingenue, hoping it would appeal to this man's fatherly instincts, if he had any. Then she continued, "And in the picture it looked just like a boy I went to school with." She waved her hands vaguely in the air, and went right on with her story, sounding foolish and scatter-brained. "And I thought, 'Can it be? Can he be Pete Kelly?' And then I came inside and took a look and I saw it wasn't."

The man's stern face relaxed. "I see."

"I know it was wrong to come into your office, but I thought I'd just sneak a look . . . I'm sorry . . ." She broke off and looked at him with innocent, pleading eyes. "Wasn't it a terrible thing to do?"

He smiled and said, "Now don't upset yourself, young lady," indicating a chair. "Have a seat and you can tell me why you're here in the first place. My recep-tionist tells me you've been waiting for me."

"I don't want to take up too much of your time, Mr. Johnson," she said, acting impressed. "After all I'm only a college student and I know you must be a very

195

busy man." She smiled and extended a hand across the desk toward him. "My name is Jane Cross and I'm doing a paper on civic responsibility for the paper at school — U. of P. — and I just wanted five minutes of your time to ask a few questions." She broke off. "I know I should have phoned for an appointment or something, but I thought I'd take a chance." She wondered how he could possibly be taken in by her story, yet he seemed to be listening very intently and his look of encouragement had her blundering on. "I've got a list of questions here . . . let me see . . ." She was looking through her briefcase in the next minute and came out with a paper she had prepared earlier that morning.

"Go right ahead," Thomas Johnson said graciously. The clock in the corner struck the half hour, nine-thirty. "I can give you ten minutes. Will that do?"

"Oh, that's wonderful," she gurgled. "Now let me see, Question No. 1 is, What led you into public office? Had you always wanted to be in some branch of government?"

He smiled benignly. "Not exactly. Years ago I had thought of being an explorer, something adventurous like that. But my father convinced me to give up my wild schemes and go to law school. That was where I first became involved with the poor people of this great American society." He added gravely, "That was what did it for me, Miss Cross. My family — the Johnsons — have always had money. I could not stand to see so many people suffering, going hungry."

Donna, who had been scratching away on her steno pad as quickly as she could, to make it appear that she was indeed taking notes, felt a surge of guilt. He sounded so sincere, she felt like a cheat, invading his office, his privacy, with what now seemed to be a childish game. Surely this fine man could have had nothing to do with the attacks on Janet. Why couldn't she have gone there in all honesty; why couldn't she have come right out and said what she really wanted? All she had to say was, "Mr. Johnson, a car owned by you tried to run my friend down. What do you know about it?"

Even now, she was tempted to confess everything to him. He was such a warm man, sitting behind his desk, trying to help her. She felt it would be safe to tell him everything. He would understand, she thought, even if she told him Janet's whole story.

"What is it, Miss Cross? You seem

197

troubled about something. Want to tell me what it is?" He waited for her answer.

That decided her. She would give him the truth. She owed him that, didn't she? What nerve to have invaded the premises of this busy, important man with such a trumped-up story. He had a wonderful face; it beamed benevolently at her, urging her on.

"I have a confession to make," she began.

Then suddenly he looked away from her and toward the door where the frigid receptionist was holding a sheaf of papers in her hand. "Mr. Johnson, the Atlanta office called for . . ." She broke off as she noticed Donna sitting there. "How did you get in here?" The words were out in a rush, and she turned apologetically to Mr. Johnson. "I asked her what she was doing here but she wouldn't tell me, Mr. Johnson. Then I had to go to the files and when I came back and didn't see her, I thought she had left." She threw a nasty look in Donna's direction.

"It's perfectly all right, Miss Gardner," he said. "This young lady is a budding journalist and I'm flattered that she thinks I'm worth interviewing for the Penn Tattler."

"I'm sorry," the receptionist said to

Donna. "If only you had told me, I wouldn't have been so rude to you."

Donna squirmed with guilt. How could she have tried to pull such a nasty trick on such nice people? She almost hated herself. She sat there, miserably wondering how to clear herself of the whole problem. Only one way to do it. Tell the whole truth.

"You don't have to apologize," she said to the young woman. "I'm the one who should apologize. I have a confession to make." In her embarrassment, her eyes shifted to the doorway through which the receptionist had just entered. As she searched for the proper words, the elevator doors opened and a tall, lean man in an overcoat stepped out. He was wearing a brimmed hat and he turned quickly and disappeared through a doorway on the far side of the reception room. A tremor ran through Donna as she realized who he was. Even though the reception room was dimly lit, she *knew*.

"You were saying . . .?" It was Mr. Johnson's voice, slightly impatient, waiting for her to finish.

"As I said, I have a confession to make." The blood pounded in her ears as she searched wildly for some way to finish the sentence. "I've interviewed, oh, lots of people, but I must confess — " she smiled brilliantly at him — "nobody ever as important as you, Mr. Johnson. And I really feel maybe my questions are too . . . simple."

"Not at all," he assured her. "There is no question of yours I wouldn't be willing to answer, young lady. That's where our citizens of tomorrow come from — the young people of today. Young people like you, asking questions."

Somehow she got through the rest of the questions on her list. If Mr. Johnson had asked her to repeat something he had said, it would have been hopeless; the mass of pothooks she was writing were meaningless. She couldn't wait to get out of there.

It was almost ten o'clock when she jumped up and said, "Well, this has been the most wonderful experience for me. How can I ever thank you, Mr. Johnson?"

He came around to her side of the desk to escort her out. "Just write a good article, Miss Cross. And be sure to send me a copy when it comes out."

"Oh, I will," she said. "I will."

Out in the street, Donna gave silent thanks for the fate that had sent the tall stranger into Mr. Johnson's office at the moment he had showed up. Whatever the connection, one thing was obvious — Mr. Johnson must know the man. Instant pictures flashed through her mind. The dark silhouette of the figure in the cemetery, in the Monmouth Inn, behind the wheel of the silver gray car that had tried to run Janet down. Flash impressions, but too terribly like the man she had just seen upstairs in the brimmed hat and overcoat to be ignored.

All right. Mr. Johnson was up to something . . . something that meant danger to Janet. What was it?

She walked slowly past the stores that were bustling with shoppers, not seeing them, only trying to figure out the mystery. How could she possibly learn anything more until she knew more about Mr. Johnson? Then it came to her. The obvious next step — the back-issue files of the Philadelphia newspapers, so she could learn all about Mr. Johnson and what made him tick.

In the back copy room of the newspaper, Donna began an operation now familiar to her. The slow and careful searching of papers on microfilm. The subject, "Thomas Wingdale Johnson, City Supervisor." The files on him were plentiful.

They went back to 1921, the year he was born, then followed his career right from there through his school years at Yale, where he had gained a Bachelor of Arts degree, where his father had gotten a law degree before him, and where he got his own LLB in 1947. There were pictures of Thomas Johnson receiving honors from various city and fraternal organizations, but these were all recent, within the past five or ten years.

She ran the file backward, and came to the announcement of the death of his father, Thomas Johnson I, in 1956. The newspaper photo of his father resembled the man whose picture she had seen in the anteroom.

Then, as the roll of film sped backward, she came to it, headlined in the lower part of the first page of the *Bulletin*, a picture illustrating the astonishing story:

Family of Donald Johnson, Financier, Dies in Switzerland Plane Crash

Then, under it, a subhead:

Father, Mother and Son Killed Instantly

and under it, still another subtitle:

Thomas Johnson II, Philadelphia Lawyer, Sole Survivor

Avidly Donna read the article. According to the paper, the Donald Johnsons had unexpectedly cut short a stay in Switzerland, chartered a private plane, and were heading home when the engine had exploded in midair, killing the pilot, co-pilot, and the plane's three occupants, the Donald Johnsons and their twenty-year-old son, Donald Johnson II.

After finishing the article, Donna read several follow-up articles printed after the tragedy. From them she learned that Thomas Wingdale Johnson II, twenty-seven years old, nephew of Donald Johnson, had inherited the entire Donald Johnson fortune.

She sat there, weighing the information. What did it mean? According to Thomas Johnson, his father had been a wealthy man in his own right. Why should it bother her that he had inherited his uncle's vast fortune? What possible connection could any of this have with Janet? She read the article again, searching for she knew not what.

Then she saw it. Not the story. The dateline on the story: "Lucerne, Switzerland, February 12, 1958."

The year Janet was born.

A small item, really, but a coincidence. Another coincidence.

Donna sat there, rubbing her forehead as if she hoped somehow the answer would pop out at her.

Was there some link, somewhere, between Thomas Johnson and his cousin Donald and Janet's mother, Ellen Willins.

Ellen Willins! Of course. She and she alone had the answer. They *must* see her. And now. Not a moment to spare.

"I can't believe it," Janet said. "A man like that would never have anything to do with the things that have been happening to me. Representative Thomas Johnson, of the State Legislature? Don't you know how crazy that sounds?"

"I don't care *how* it sounds," Donna said. "It was *his* car that was used when they tried to run you down — whoever it was. And I swear to you, Janet, it was the same man in his office that we saw in the hotel that night in Baltimore."

Janet shook her head stubbornly. "What would they have to do with me? People high in government, millionaires, people like that?"

"Janet, I won't argue it with you. I just think we have to go up to see your mother. That means we have to make a phone call to your Uncle Richard. Will you do it?"

"Yes," Janet said. "I want to see my mother — but not for the reasons you're talking about. When do you want me to call him?"

"Now. Come on. We'll get his number from information."

Janet took a deep breath. "Okay — I'm ready."

Donna waited outside the phone booth, out of earshot of the conversation, but close enough to see Janet's forehead beaded with perspiration. *I hope he believes her*, Donna thought. What a shock to come at anyone over the telephone — the voice of a young adult, the abandoned child of his sister — his niece. After all these years. Maybe he didn't know of Janet's existence. Maybe he did, but thought he and his family would never hear of the child again. Drama on a high scale, entering his life so abruptly.

Janet spoke for four or five minutes; Donna watched her earnest face, flushed with strain. Then Janet flung the door of the booth open and said to Donna, "Can we go to New York City tomorrow morning to meet him?"

Donna nodded wildly and said, "Yes. Of course!"

Janet turned back, closed the door and continued to speak for a few minutes. Then she hung up the phone and just sat inside the booth, visibly wilting, lost in thought, until Donna tapped lightly with her fingernails on the glass door.

Janet came out and said, "Donna, he sounds so suspicious. I had to talk him into it. He said there was no way I could be his sister's child. But he'll see me and try to straighten me out, since I seem to have so much information about his family." She ran a hand through her damp hair and said, "Donna, I'm wiped out. I swear, this is more than I can handle."

Donna said, "You're just emotionally strung out. What you need is a picker-upper. Let's take a slow stroll down to Pagano's and shovel some energy into you. And I don't mean cannoli bursting with vanilla cream and all that goo. I mean a great big antipasto full of raw vegetables and cheese and salami and tunafish."

Janet looked at her pleadingly. "And if I eat all that grass and stuff, please, can't I have *half* a cream puff?"

"You're hopeless," Donna said, laughing and linking her arm through Janet's. "Yes, you can," she said, beaming at her friend like an indulgent mother with an infant beside her. "Then we'll go home and tuck you beddy-bye, because tomorrow is a big day. We're going to the big city to meet your Uncle Richard. Now will you behave?"

"I'll twy," Janet said. "Weally, I will, Mommy."

As they entered Pagano's a few moments later, Donna thought: She's come a long way, she really has. What she needs more than anything in this world is to see Ellen Willins.

Chapter 14

They met him in the lobby of the Plaza Hotel. They waited together, and then they saw a sturdily built figure coming toward them.

"I'm Richard Willins," he said. Then as she nodded, he looked at Janet. "And you're...?"

"Janet." She said no last name.

Donna was surprised to see that there was little or no resemblance between Janet and her Uncle Richard. Janet's long brown smooth hair and light blue eyes in no way were identifiable with his bright dark brown eyes and swarthy complexion. He was a good-looking man, with clearly Latin or Mediterranean background. The same doubts were going through his mind, for he said:

"I don't have to tell you how surprised I was to get your phone call. I think maybe you two young ladies are barking up the wrong tree. We better go someplace and talk."

He led them across the main lobby to the central court, where there were comfortable chairs around small tables, with dark green potted palms separating each cluster of tables from the other. They had privacy enough so that Richard Willins didn't bother to lower his voice after they were seated and had ordered their drinks.

Looking directly at Janet, he said, "Before I get my sister and her family all upset, you've got to explain to me and show me positive proof of what you told me on the phone last night."

"Don't worry," Donna said. "We wouldn't have thought of coming if we didn't know for sure that Janet is Ellen Willins' daughter. I can't tell you, Mr. Willins, how much time we've spent making sure of the facts ... almost two months of hard, grinding investigation. We've been through all the official records that we could find in the City Hall, the courthouse, even the children's home Janet came from."

At a look from Donna, Janet took out of the briefcase the material they had so painstakingly gathered the past six weeks.

She handed them to her Uncle Richard, who took them with a skeptical look on his face.

But his attitude changed visibly as he read through paper after paper, beginning with "The Adoption of Baby Girl Willins by Joseph and Mary Bryson." When he had finished, he said nothing, but just sat and looked at Janet.

"What is it?" she said. "You still don't believe me?"

He said, "I have to believe you. There's a whole lot of things — I'll tell you in a minute . . ." he gulped, then went on. "Now that I take a good look at you, you look like my sister. She's got that kind of eyebrows, the same as you, and her hair, I remember how it was. Yours is just like hers. I take after my father's side of the family." He pushed his glass aside. "I know you're telling the truth. You're a Willins, all right."

Donna reached over and grabbed Janet's hand, who clutched back in an almost iron grip.

"Donna, Donna! Can you believe it?" Her eyes shone with tears of relief.

"I believe it," Donna said. "Now let's hear what else your uncle has to say."

Richard Willins had few facts to give

them, but they fit in too perfectly to be ignored.

"Your mother, my sister Ellen, is three years younger than I am. That means I was twenty-one years old when she had you. And that explains something I've never been able to understand." He hesitated, and shook his head incredulously. "It's hard for me to take it all in, but I'll try to figure it out. I was in the service back then — from 1956 to 1958. Stationed in Colorado. That was when my mother and father told me Ellen was suffering from a nervous condition. I swear, I couldn't understand it." His dark eyes clouded over. "Ellen was never the nervous type. My mother and father were real strict, you know?" He laughed abashedly. "Tell the truth, it's why I went into service, to get away from all their rules and regulations. But it never seemed to bother Ellen. At least until she got sick."

"It must have been a big surprise," Donna said.

He nodded. "I was with the Air Force — and we were going to be sent overseas, to Korea. I wanted to come home for a last visit, but my father talked me out of it." His mouth quirked. "I never understood it — not until now."

211

"You think my mother was pregnant with me, and your family was trying to keep it a secret — even from you?" Janet said.

"That's all I can think. They told me Ellen was under treatment for her nerves. Then, when I was in Korea they sent me a letter saying Ellen had gone out to a special sort of a rest home in Baltimore." He looked meaningfully at Janet, who nodded. Then he went on, "That's where the home you were finally put in was, right? And I don't know what happened after that. You'll find out when you talk to my sister Ellen — your mother."

Janet said, "You mean you will tell her about me — let me see her? You mean it?"

"Of course. What else can I do? You've convinced me." He looked at her appraisingly. "Listen, kid, you deserve a break after all you must have gone through to find out this much."

"Thank you, thanks so much," Janet said.

"I don't know how my sister is going to take this. You know, she's married, to a nice guy, and she's got two kids with him. I'm sure she never told him or anyone about you." Janet looked down at her hands. "But don't worry, I'll find a way to talk to her and find out if she wants to see you." He cleared his throat. "That sounds kind of cruel, I guess. But this is bound to be a big shock to her."

Donna said, "This has been a big shock to you too, Mr. Willins."

Janet looked directly at him, and said softly, "It certainly has been. And you've been very understanding."

He said, almost harshly, "Why not? You're my niece, aren't you?"

They stood up, and he said, "I'll call you as soon as I can talk to my sister alone. I have to wait until there's no one in the house." Janet nodded. He said, "I'll call you the minute I know anything."

They all shook hands and said good-bye. Elated, Donna and Janet walked out of the hotel lobby and down the steps into the street.

"Come on," Donna said. "We've got to get a train back to Philadelphia. If we hurry, we can make the one o'clock Metro-liner."

They took a taxi to Penn Station and just made it to the train platform in time.

"Janet, my love," Donna said. "Let's go into the dining car and celebrate. We've earned it."

"You bet," Janet said. "I can't wait to hear from him. When do you think he'll call?"

213

Donna thought a moment. "He's a pretty dynamic man, Janet. I guess firemen have to make quick decisions and take quick action. I wouldn't be surprised if you heard from him tomorrow or the next day. Maybe even tonight."

That was when the call came. They were back in their apartment, washing up the dinner dishes, when the phone rang.

"I got lucky, Janet," her Uncle Richard said. "I got my sister long enough to tell her to call me from an outside phone, and she did. She made some excuse to leave the house, and then called me right back."

Janet waited, afraid to speak.

"I broke the news as best I could," he said. "But it wasn't easy for her. She started to cry, right on the phone."

Janet said, "What did she say?"

"She wants to see you."

Janet's heart jumped. "When?"

"Can you come up this Saturday? I can meet you there and take you to her."

In a few minutes, Janet hung up and said to Donna, with eyes shining, "Donna! It's all set! She'll see me! On Saturday, *I'm going to see my mother!*"

Chapter 15

"What you are not doing is going up to Vermont alone. I won't hear of it," Pete said. They were sitting in his car, which was parked a few feet from Donna's apartment house.

"Great," Donna said. "But you don't have to issue orders. Janet and I have talked it over and, believe it or not, we think you might even be a help if you came along."

Pete assumed an injured air. "What do you mean? Are you questioning my male supremacy? My superior strength and mental agility?"

Donna punched him lightly on the arm. "We want you because something crazy is going on and Thomas Johnson, big wheel, is someplace right in there."

"Where?" Pete asked.

"I don't know."

"I can't believe that a man who is so

civic-minded and has done so much for people could be mixed up in anything like what's been happening to you two. Why, that's a criminal offense — I mean, any one of those things could send a man to jail for ten, twenty years." Pete shook his head unbelievingly. "Whatever way this Johnson is mixed up in Janet's life, I refuse to believe he was behind any of those things you seem to think he is."

"Then keep on refusing to believe it," Donna said, "but drive us up to Vermont this weekend and we'll be grateful for your company — and protection. Not because you're a man, but because three are better than two."

"What time do you want to leave?"

"Let me see. The appointment with Janet's mother is for eleven o'clock in the morning on Saturday. I guess it all depends on how long it takes to get to Vermont from here."

Pete said, "Well, it's roughly four hundred miles. That's at least six or seven hours."

"Then we'll have to drive up the day before and stay someplace that isn't too expensive."

"I've already thought of that," Pete said grinning. "I know a great place. Very

216

cheap — and only a couple of miles away from Stowe."

"And it happens to be a ski lodge, I'll bet," Donna said, "with a ski lift and a couple of jazzy runs and complete equipment for hire and . . . what else, Pete?"

"All right, you've convinced me. You're the greatest detective since Sherlock Holmes. But this time, the treat's on me. Maybe Saturday will be heavy going for Janet when she sees her mother for the first time, but the day before we're going to have some fun at Tuxedo Lodge. Got that?"

"Got it." Donna was about to say something to the effect that it was pretty sweet of Pete to be making these arrangements for them, but she never had a chance. He pulled her to him and as they kissed, Donna realized once again how deeply she cared for him.

Tuxedo Lodge was not exactly a Hollywood-type ski lodge. It was much smaller and much more rugged than the beautiful ones in the movies. It was a long, low building with rough-hewn, wooden beamed walls, ceilings and floors, and the rooms had built-in bunk beds that the guests had to make up themselves. The main lobby was nothing more than one big room with a fireplace, a hi-fi set, records, a few books, and some rustic chairs and benches to sit on.

"Not exactly luxury," Pete said, grinning, "but the prices are really low, and..."

"Don't apologize," Donna said. "We're thrilled that you're treating us to it. And it's close enough to where we're going tomorrow."

"That goes for me too." Janet looked at Pete affectionately. "I mean, as long as you don't try to make me go skiing."

Pete laughed. "You think I'm out of my mind? With your ankle not even healed? You can watch Donna and me from the sidelines."

"I'm not leaving Janet alone," Donna said. "Not for one minute. Besides, I can get all the skiing I need back in Pennsylvania."

"Not the kind they have at Silver Ridge," Pete said. "They've got this great cable car that takes you up to the top of a mountain — the most spectacular view you ever saw." He shrugged as Donna shook her head. "Okay, you two take the cable car up and you can watch while I try the slalom run."

218

"Sounds good," Donna said. "When do we start?"

"I've signed us all in, and I found out how to get to Silver Ridge. Why don't you two run up to your room and stash your things away while I fill the car up with gas? But don't take too long because there's only about two hours left till sundown and it's a ten-mile drive from here."

"Come on, Janet," Donna said, heading for the stairs. "He'll never forgive us if we cost him even five minutes of his precious skiing."

A half hour later, Pete and the girls arrived at Silver Ridge.

"Now this is what I call a glamour ski lodge," Donna said.

"Magnificent," Janet agreed. "How did you find out about it, Pete?"

"It's *the* outstanding resort in the whole state," he said. "Well, we'd better get over to the cable car."

They crossed the snow-laden slope to a clump of barren trees, where a few skiers were waiting for the cable car.

Janet took one look up at the mountaintop where the cable car had just started its descent, and her face turned white.

"What's the matter?" Pete asked. "Forgot something?"

Donna studied her friend's face a moment. "No, I think she remembered something." Then she asked Janet, "You're afraid to go up that high. Right?"

Janet said miserably, "I can't help it. Just the thought of being up in that tiny cable car has me frantic. Look!" She held out her hands, palms upward. They were wet with perspiration, even in the cold air. "I can't help it. I get this way looking out a window on the twentieth story of an office building."

Donna said to Pete, "You should have seen her when we saw that movie, *Towering Inferno*. Even in the theater her hands got wringing wet and she almost passed out."

Pete put his hands on Janet's shoulders. "I think we'd better ground you for the duration. That okay with you?"

Janet said gratefully, "It sure is. Thanks, Pete."

"I'll go back with you," Donna said. But then she saw the unhappy expression on Pete's face. "You want me to watch your slalom act, right? You'll never forgive me if I don't?"

"No, it's okay," Pete said.

Donna stood undecided a moment. Then she said, "Listen, Janet, do you mind waiting for us in the lodge?"

"Not at all," Janet said. "I'm freezing. I'll have some hot chocolate and wait till you get back."

Pete's face lit up like Christmas tree. "Great. We'll walk you back," he said.

"Not necessary," Janet said.

"Yes, it is," Pete persisted. "Your ankle's still not perfect, and it's icy underfoot."

When Pete and Donna got back to the place the cable car left from, a man in his fifties, in heavy mackinaw and woolen cap, said as they approached, "I guess you people ain't heard about the big doings tonight."

"What's that?" Pete asked.

"It's Hoedown night — biggest to-do in these parts in the whole year. Ain't you noticed? There's nobody goin' up the slope anymore — not since that last trip. Not on the ski lift, and not on the car. They're all gettin' ready for the shindig tonight. Sure you want to go?"

Donna looked at Pete, who said, "I've wanted to go down Fox Mountain since I saw pictures of it back in '74. It's where the Olympic skiers train, isn't it?"

"Right you are, young man. Matter of fact, the slalom run's set up right now for them." The man in the mackinaw opened the side door of the cable car. "In you go."

He slammed the door shut and waved cheerily as the cable car started its ascent toward the peak.

As the car made its way slowly across the abyss between the two points, the view was breathtaking. Higher and higher the two went, spellbound by the magnificent sweep of snow-topped crags highlighted against dark valleys plunging thousands of feet below.

Pete said, "Have you ever seen anything like this?"

"It's spectacular," Donna said. "But I wish we'd hurry and get to the top. I *hate* the idea of Janet alone in the lodge. Don't ask me why."

Pete put a comforting arm around her. "I don't blame you, honey. So much has happened to the two of you, it would be stupid not to think about it. But what can possibly happen to Janet while we're gone? Nobody even knows that she's here at all."

Donna shuddered slightly. "That's what Janet and I thought when we went down to Baltimore. And someone tried to run her over. Remember?"

By this time they were approaching the top. At a small wooden shed that housed the cable-car motor, a man stood waiting. He was dressed in heavy winter clothing and his cheeks were rosy with the cold, making him look like a benign Santa Claus. He said, "Well, I never did expect to see any more folks today. If it wasn't for you folks, I could go home."

Pete, reading the old man's mind, reached into his pocket and took out a dollar bill. "Thanks. We certainly appreciate your staying here. My girl friend will be going down in just a few minutes. Then you'll be through."

"Not so," the old man said, his eyes squinting down the long slope. "If I'm not mistaken, there's somebody else waitin' to come up." He sighed, then looked at the bill in his hand. "Well, this is very nice of you, young fella."

As Pete and Donna started toward the roped off area where the run began, he called after them, "You going down the east slope or the slalom?"

"The slalom," Pete said.

"Better watch it, then. It's late and the last man out left ten minutes ago. You'll be alone."

"Don't worry," Pete said, "I'm a pretty good skier."

"And I'll keep an eye on him till he's almost at the bottom," Donna said.

The old man said, "That's a good idea. Can't be too careful." He waved a hand and said, "Well, I'd better get this car down to the bottom. Looks like you'll have company after all. But I tell you one thing — this one comin' up is positively the last."

The sun was beginning to drop behind heavy snow clouds, but the brilliance of the snowy slopes still reflected bright light as Donna and Pete trudged up the remaining forty or fifty yards to the starting place for the slalom.

"You sure you want to do this?" Donna asked.

"Baby, I didn't come all this way to ride that cable car back down." Pete leaned over and kissed her lightly. "Don't be such a worry wart. It'll take me no more than seven or eight minutes to get to the bottom. When you see me at the halfway post, you get back on the cable car and I'll meet you where it lets off."

He got into his skis quickly, and with a final kiss, left her standing there in a flurry of snow the wind was whipping up. He took off, yelled, "Watch this!" and swooped down a steep incline as Donna thought, he's like a kid showing off to his mama. He turned back as he rounded the first post to look at her and waved a pole, and she waved back. Then he was swooping down rapidly among the posts in a swift plunge toward the base far below. She was so intent watching him, admiring his style and his courage, that she never heard or saw the cable car coming back up to the landing place on the level off to her right.

When she could no longer see Pete's racing figure against the gray-white landscape, she made her way gingerly down the slope toward the cable car. An icy blast was blowing up from the caverns below, and she shivered with the cold as she descended the last few feet. Approaching the cable car, she was surprised to see that the old man with the rosy cheeks was gone. In his place was a much taller man, dressed in a sleek ski outfit, black from head to toe, that included a black ski mask covering his entire head, leaving only slits for his eyes and mouth. He looked like Death incarnate.

Donna stopped dead in her tracks. She started to back away but it was too late. With the grunt of a wild animal, the black figure lunged toward her. She started to run but the man was wearing ski shoes and was much too fast for her. As he seized her from behind, she gave one last desperate look down the slope and screamed, "Pete!" But it was hopeless. There was no one to see, no one to hear; she was alone in the snowy void with this monstrous creature.

He said nothing as he pinned her with her arms twisted behind her back. He half-dragged, half-pushed her across the icy slope, up, up, further away from the cable-car housing. Where was he taking her?

It was a nightmare, and she was living in it. Then she realized what he had in mind. Of course — it could be only one thing. He was taking her to the top to shove her off the cliff . . . the one that dropped thousands of feet to the valley below. The one she and Pete had seen from the cable car on the way up.

She did not waste her strength in screaming. Who could hear? There was no one to hear, no one to know. There were so few feet to go. Her mind was racing madly. A kaleidoscope of impressions flashed past her eyes — her home, her mother, her family, Pete, Janet. She was going helplessly to her death — a hideous death, alone here on the deserted mountain peak, with no one, nothing to help.

If only he hadn't such an iron grasp on her. Her arms were pinned together at the wrists and she felt as if they were being pulled out of the sockets. She had to restrain herself from blacking out from the pain. She bit her lip till it bled, not even knowing, so intense was the hurt in her arms, her shoulders. Then came a flash of the afternoon Pete had shown her the throw. Her mind, flashing in and out of consciousness, opened like a shutter. Yes, that was it. Again a wave of black swept her brain, but then a flash of bright consciousness. What was it? The arms? No use. Can't move. The legs? The feet? No hold, too much ice, too much snow. Then what? Pete's face now, his voice, telling the kids, "Go for the throat!" Mind shuttering in and out, in and out, a black and white movie, old movie, black and white.

"Go for the throat . . ." How? Head. My head . . . throat . . . his throat . . . Can do it? Got . . . to . . . try. Almost . . . at . . . top. Mustn't let him . . . push me over.

They were at the very peak now. With horrified eyes she saw the wide open abyss before her, the gray-black pool of nothingness that meant the end of the world, her world. She breathed a silent prayer as she mustered all her strength and in one crashing wrench, jolted her head full force backward toward the man. The pain in her shoulders was unbearable, but she forced herself to go through the motion

again, and this time she hit her mark —
his throat. She heard a heavy rasping
sound, a guttural rip from his throat, and
he released her and dropped to the ground
at the very edge of the precipice. Before
she could make a move to stop him, he
slid over the precipice and plunged out
of sight.

She stood there, rooted in shock, looking at the place where her attacker had gone over. She would have to force herself to go to the edge and look over. She dreaded the thought of it, of seeing, knowing, what had happened to him. If only Pete would come...

She heard the crunch of footsteps behind her. She turned and in the deepening dusk saw two figures making their way up the slope toward her. Pete — and Janet.

"Pete!" his name burst from her lips.

In a moment he was beside her, holding her, asking, "Are you all right? We saw it from the cable car!"

She nodded, and let herself go into the warm safety of his arms. She saw Janet looking at her worriedly, and said, "It's okay, Jan. I'm all right."

Then she looked fearfully toward the

Chapter 16

She stood there, rooted in shock, looking at the place where her attacker had gone over. She would have to force herself to go to the edge and look over. She dreaded the thought of it, of seeing, knowing, what had happened to him. If only Pete would come...

She heard the crunch of footsteps behind her. She turned and in the deepening dusk saw two figures making their way up the slope toward her. Pete — and Janet.

"Pete!" his name burst from her lips.

In a moment he was beside her, holding her, asking, "Are you all right? We saw it from the cable car!"

She nodded, and let herself go into the warm safety of his arms. She saw Janet looking at her worriedly, and said, "It's okay, Jan. I'm all right."

Then she looked fearfully toward the

precipice over which the figure in black had disappeared.

Pete read the fear in her face and said, "Stay here with Janet. I'll take a look."

The two girls watched as Pete made his way on the icy ground to the edge. There he dropped carefully on one knee, and, bracing himself, looked over and down. About ten feet below, on a small icy ledge jutting out from the sheer mountain wall, there lay a crumpled figure clothed in black.

Pete came back to them and told them, "I think he's still alive. Of course I can't tell. I'd better go to the cable-car housing and phone for a rescue squad."

As he walked off, Donna turned to Janet and said, "I don't understand. How did you know?"

"That you were in trouble?" Now Janet was helping her down the slope. Donna was grateful for her support. "It happened after you and Pete left me in the lodge. I saw you go, and then a man in a black ski suit ran past me. I don't know why, but I went to the door to see why he was in such a hurry."

"Was that when Pete and I were going up in the cable car?" Donna asked.

"Yes. But he was too late to catch that car. He had to take the next one."

"What did you do?" Donna said.

"I wasn't sure who he was," Janet said. "I went after him anyway, but my ankle slowed me down. I knew Pete would be skiing down in a few minutes, and I knew there had to be a man on duty up at the top, operating the cable car." She shook her head, and her eyes clouded. "I didn't realize how long it would take Pete to slalom down the slope. I swear, Donna, it seemed like hours, though it was only six or seven minutes. When I got Pete and we both were riding up the mountain, we could see what was happening — at times, I mean, depending on where the car was, and it seemed like centuries till we got to the top."

By this time, the two were at the cable-car housing. They entered and found Pete just hanging up the wall phone, while beside him, rubbing his head, the rosy-cheeked operator greeted them ruefully.

"Nearly did for me, he did," he said. "That was some knock on the head I got." He lifted a coffee mug that smelled suspiciously of brandy to his lips. "You okay, young lady?" he asked Donna. And when she nodded, he said, "Ain't never had a thing like this happen afore. Not in all my years. Who could've done a rotten stunt like that, I wonder?"

"I think we have a very good idea," Donna said.

An hour later, back at Tuxedo Lodge, the three friends were comfortably ensconced on a low sofa in front of the big fireplace in the lobby. A fire was blazing merrily away on the hearth, and from time to time, Pete was removing a long toasting fork laden with browned, melted marshmallows, handing some to Donna and Janet, keeping some for himself.

"It's lucky he wasn't killed," Pete said. "Although that's what he intended for you, Donna. He's also lucky the rescue crew went down and got him out in a lift basket so fast."

"Do they know who he is?" Donna said.

"No, he's in too bad shape for questioning. They found no identification on him, which is odd in itself," Pete said.

"What about laundry marks on his clothing? Or dry cleaning ones?" Donna asked.

"Good girl," Pete said. "That's just what the police are checking out — the laundry mark on his shirt, but since they don't know what city he comes from, it can take a long time."

Donna said, "Tell them to try Philadelphia first."

"That's what I told them," Janet said. "I told the police I thought the man in black was after the wrong person, because we were wearing practically the same outfit — our blue and gold U of P sweaters and dark ski pants and with our heads covered in scarves. It's easy to mistake one of us for the other, especially if we're not too close together."

"If I ever get to open a detective agency, I'll hire you for an assistant," Donna said.

"No, thanks," Janet said firmly. "It's not for me."

Pete said seriously, "It's not for you, either, Donna."

"If you tell me it's man's work, I'll brain you," Donna said.

"We'll discuss it another time," Pete said. "Right now, we're going to get some food into you. Janet has a big date tomorrow."

"Yes," Donna said. "A very important date. You sure you want me to go with you, Janet?"

Janet said, "I wish you would. I'll tell Mrs. Requena — I mean, my mother — that you're my best friend. She'll understand."

I wonder, Donna thought. I wonder what kind of woman she is.

* * *

233

Later that night, when they were in bed, Janet said, "I'm scared, Donna. Suppose she doesn't like me?"

"Suppose she doesn't? How about your own feelings?" Donna said.

"What I feel, more than anything else, is that I want to know the truth. I want to know how she met my father, I want to know who he is, and I've got to know why she gave me up. Did she want to — or did someone make her do it?" Janet bit her fingernail anxiously. "No matter what happens tomorrow, I've got to know!"

Donna said, "Go ahead, I'm listening. Say whatever you like. We've been on this search so long, Jan — and yet you've never really told me what you're hoping for when you meet your mother."

"That's because until a few days ago, I never really thought we'd find her."

"What do you expect? That the two of you will take one look at each other and just run into each other's arms?" Donna waited for her friend to answer.

It took several minutes before Janet said: "Yes — yes! That's my dream! I don't care if it sounds crazy. Why should it? I'm her flesh and blood. If I had a baby — whether I was married or not — I'd never give it up! Maybe all these years she's been thinking of me — the same way I've been thinking of her these past few years." She shifted in her chair. "I tell you, Donna, my mother and father — the Brysons — were wonderful to me. You know that. But still, knowing I was adopted, someplace deep inside of me I don't feel I have any roots. I know my life really began someplace else, with some other people, way before the adoption agency gave me to the Brysons. That's what I'm looking for — my *real* roots." She brushed away the tears that started to come. "I'm not going to waste this meeting tomorrow. I want to know everything!"

Donna said, "Listen, Janet, suppose you find out — something bad? Then what?"

Janet said, "Then at least I'll know the truth. Don't you see? All I want to know is what really happened nineteen years ago . . . what was going on in my life that landed me in a children's home. I feel like someone with amnesia . . . with a blank space in life that I can't fill in." Janet was getting calmer now.

Donna reached over and took her hand. "Tomorrow, Jan — tomorrow you'll find out."

Chapter 17

The house was simple, unpretentious. A small front yard banked with snow led to a porch unprotected from the elements. They brushed the snow from their boots on a small straw doormat and before Janet could push the bell, the door opened and there was Richard Willins.

"Come in," he said. "I'm glad you're here. My sister is waiting for you."

The living room was dark; green shades had been drawn against the daylight. In a corner of the room, a short, thick-waisted woman dressed in navy-blue stood waiting. Her features were plain, and she looked older than her age. She put her hand out toward Janet, and Janet crossed the room nervously and took it. For a moment they stood there like that, the woman and the girl, strangers, looking at each other.

Then the woman said, indicating the sofa beside her, "Sit down . . . Janet."

Janet sat down and Ellen Requena took a seat beside her. Donna took a seat across the room, near Richard Willins, who was standing in the doorway, watching silently. If there had been a moment when the two women might have embraced, it was past now. Janet sat uncomfortably on a flowered cretonne sofa, as her mother looked long and hard at her with sombre, dark-brown eyes. The older woman's face was alien to Janet, who felt self-conscious in the plaid pantsuit she had chosen for this occasion.

After a long silence, her mother said, "So you found me." She twisted a fold of her navy dress between her fingers. "I always expected that someday it would happen."

She started to cry. But after a moment she got control of herself and said, "I always thought someday the phone would ring or someone would come to my house, and at least I would know what happened to you."

Janet said, "I'll tell you about myself, if you want."

Her mother said, "Oh yes, I want to know."

It took only a short while for Janet to explain about her life with the Brysons, the death of Mr. Bryson, and all the details she felt her mother would expect to hear.

When she had finished, her mother said, "I want to tell you everything that happened. I really do. I know I owe it to you." Her lips trembled, but she made herself go on.

"I met your father in the summer, Janet. He came from Philadelphia, but he was studying in Baltimore. I was working in the library, and he used to come there." She sighed, remembering. "We went out for only two or three months, but we were in love." She looked at Janet with those sad brown eyes. "Your father came from very good people. If he had lived, he would have married me."

Across the room, Donna's heart lurched. She strained to hear Mrs. Requena's next words.

"I — I became pregnant." Under her dark skin, she blushed. "When I found out, I sent him a letter. He was in Europe with his mother and father. And then it happened." Her voice broke harshly. "The accident. He was killed. They were all killed." She couldn't go on.

That's it, Donna thought — the missing

piece in the puzzle. She didn't need to hear the name Mrs. Requena said next:

"Donald Johnson. That was your father, Janet. So handsome, and he died so young. Only twenty years old." She was crying again.

Richard Willins was watching his sister closely from the doorway. He's wondering if all this is too much emotion for her, Donna thought. She was afraid he'd call a halt to the visit. But he remained silent as Mrs. Requena continued:

"Donald was coming home to marry me. I have the letter — here." She fumbled in her plain black purse and brought out an old faded letter in an envelope yellowed by time. "I want you to have it," she said, handing it to Janet.

Janet said, "Then my father died — before I was born?"

"Yes," her mother said. "And that's why I had to give you up." She shifted in her seat. "When my parents found out I was pregnant, they were so angry. I didn't dare tell them who the father was — what was the use? He was dead. He couldn't give my baby a name."

"What did you do?" Janet asked softly.

"They sent me to a shelter for unwed mothers, down in Georgia. When my time came, I went by taxi alone to the hospital.

No one came to visit me when you were born. My mother and father were too angry — too ashamed."

Janet reached out a hand and touched her arm. "It must have been awful for you."

Her mother was silent for a long moment. Then she said, "I'm sorry. It makes me feel so bad to remember." Her hands pulled at a crumpled handkerchief. "After a week in the hospital, I went back to the shelter for four months, so I could nurse you." She added, "You were a beautiful baby, Janet. You had a wonderful smile. I tried to get my parents to come and see you, but they wouldn't."

"What did you do then?" Janet asked.

"I didn't want to give you up, so I put you in a foster home for children in a little town outside of Baltimore so I could be near you. My mother said I could come home to live. I took a job in a store and every weekend I visited you. Once, I even got my father to come and see you. But my mother — your grandmother — never would. She was very strict."

"How long was I in the foster home?" Janet asked.

"Until you were nine months old. It broke my heart to see you in a home, with all those children who had no families."

She shook her head sadly. "I knew you needed a good home — a real home. Then you got sick, and the doctor said it was because you needed to be living with a family that would love you and take care of you. My mother still wouldn't let me bring you home. I didn't know what to do. The people in the agency told me you would go to very good people." She sighed heavily. "I signed the papers. They would never tell me where you went, or how you were. It was like a part of me died when they took you away from me."

From the doorway, Richard Willins called over, "Ellen! Are you all right? Isn't this too much for you?"

"No," she said. "I want her to know." She turned to Janet. "Then time went on, and when I was twenty-one, I met Mr. Requena. I — I never told him about you. He is a very strict man, like my parents. He would never forgive me." Her brow furrowed. "But he is very good to me and we have two children, your half-brother and half-sister."

Her cheeks were getting flushed now. "The adoption people told me that when I got married again, I would forget all about the baby I gave up. It isn't true. Every time I passed a woman in the street with a daughter, I thought, 'Is that mine?

241

Is that my little girl?' " She blinked back tears. "Oh, how I wish it all didn't have to have happened."

Janet reached over impulsively and put her arm around her mother. "I'm sorry for all the trouble you had." Somehow she could not bring herself to say the word "Mother" to this strange, sad woman. For Janet realized, even as she tried to comfort her, that they were strangers. They had lived eighteen years apart, the child separated at ten months from the mother, and there was no shared experience, no continuity. None at all.

Mrs. Requena made everyone come into the kitchen where she had set out a tray of sandwiches and a platter of cake and cookies. She urged them to eat, but neither Janet nor Donna were hungry.

"I wish I could have made something special," Mrs. Requena explained, "but my family will be coming home soon. I don't want them to get suspicious about anything." She looked anxiously at Janet. "You understand?"

"Yes," Janet said, to reassure her, but inside she felt deep pity for this frightened woman with her anxious eyes, her birdlike timidity.

When the time came to part, Janet and her mother embraced briefly. But it was clear to both of them that this meeting had been only a painful coming together of two people whose paths had finally crossed; a meeting that had given them the answers to questions that had remained unanswered for almost two decades. Now that the details had been filled in, each knew their paths were unlikely to cross again.

Night was beginning to fall and the headlights of Pete's car were beaming through a flurry of large, pale snowflakes to the narrow strip of road ahead. The ice under the tires made driving hazardous, and Pete paid careful attention to his driving. In the back of the darkened car, Donna sat quietly listening as Janet sorted out the events of a day that had been perhaps the most momentous in her life so far.

"All I keep thinking is — 'the poor woman.' It's hard for me to think of her as my mother. She stopped being my mother eighteen years ago, when she gave me away." Her eyes deepened. "She must have had a lot of spunk, once, to put up the battle she did that first year, to keep me. I mean, according to what she told me, it was her mother who wouldn't come to see me, her own little granddaughter. It was

243

her mother who told her she couldn't come home with a baby. And it was her mother who made her give me up."

"She must have been like a rock, your grandmother," Donna said. "I don't know how anyone could be so hard on her own daughter."

"Well, we'll never know. My grandmother has been dead almost ten years. But one thing I know, just from seeing my mother today, and that is — whatever courage or spirit my mother had back then, her mother killed it. Forever."

As Janet sat back in her seat, Donna studied her face. It was astonishing to see how the expression on Janet's face had changed. The strain and uncertainty were gone.

Donna said, "You look different, Janet. Do you feel different?"

"Do I?" She drew a deep breath. "I can't tell you how it feels, Donna, knowing the truth. At last I know about my family, that I'm healthy, they're all healthy people. Maybe I was expecting my mother to be some kind of a princess." She stopped, unable to make a joke. She said, "The poor woman. I guess we won't be seeing each other much. It would be too awful for her if her husband found out about me now." She said softly, "But it's so good to know. To know that she once loved me very much even though she had to give me up."

Donna sat silently. Janet said, "Now what I want to do more than anything is see my mother — my real mother, the one who brought me up all my life. I just want to tell her how much I love her and my father for all they did for me."

For a long moment neither girl said anything. Up front, Pete, who had only caught snatches of the conversation, thought, whatever is going on back there, it must be okay. Janet sounds good.

"You just said you thought that when you found your mother, Jan, you'd discover she was a princess or something. I think you may get a big surprise to learn exactly who your father was," Donna said.

"What do you mean?" Janet asked.

Donna said, "Your Uncle Richard said you look like your mother. Well, I'll admit the way your hair grows back from your forehead, and the coloring of your hair and eyes are the same — but you really don't look like her at all. As I sat there watching you both — I couldn't hear anything, Jan, and didn't want to unless you wanted to tell me — anyway, as I watched you with her, I suddenly knew who you looked like."

"What do you mean?" Janet asked. "I don't understand."

"It can only be one person, Janet," Donna said earnestly. "When I was in Thomas Johnson's office, I saw this big portrait — and then inside on his table there were these photographs, of a woman and man and a little boy, and then one of a twenty or twenty-one year old man, and now I know who he was. Your father."

"What?" Janet shook her head incredulously. "Do you know what you're saying? How could you know that?"

"Because you look just like him, Janet. Like him and his father — your grandfather."

"I can't believe all these things are happening to me," Janet said.

"Well, believe it. Maybe part of you is Willins — but you're a Johnson. You're the daughter of Donald Johnson II." Then, as she saw Janet open her purse, Donna said, "That's right. The letter."

They snapped on the overhead light in the car, and together they read what was written in a dark blue ink on faded yellow stationery:

Your letter just reached me, my dear Ellen. I have told my parents about the baby. They were upset, as can be expected, but they have agreed that you and I should be married. They know I love you very much. We are leaving on Friday, the 13th. I have written to my cousin — he's the family lawyer — and he will be in touch with you to see if you need anything before we get back. In the meantime, I send you all my love and can't wait to see you again.

Don

"Friday the 13th," Janet said softly. "And he never got back to America." She hestitated. "I wonder whether the lawyer ever got in touch with my mother."

"You may be sure that he didn't. Look, Janet," Donna said earnestly, "don't you realize what this all means?" Janet shook her head. "Your father was the son of a very rich man — a millionaire. Look," she said again, indicating the letterhead the note was written on. Her finger indicated "Hotel Excelsior, Lugano, Switzerland. A Johnson chain of hotels, Donald Johnson I, President."

"My grandfather," Janet said, finding the words strange on her lips.

"Right, honey. And also *Thomas Johnson's* uncle! Probably the sole heir to Donald Johnson's fortune, since Donald's wife and son were killed at the same time."

"How can you know all this?" Janet said.

"I don't *know* all the details, Janet. But that's how it's got to be. The minute we get back to Philadelphia, I'm asking John Harbaugh to check it all out."

Chapter 18

When they pulled up in front of the house, Abbey, who had heard them, was waiting for them in the entrance. She waved a welcome delicately, the long sleeves of her green silk kimono blowing briskly in the cold wind.

Donna said, "It's great to see you, Madame Butterfly. Wait'll you hear all our news."

"Wait'll you hear mine," Abbey said, going to the polished mahogany table in the entrance hall and picking up a telegraph form. "Look at this." With a long gold-lacquered fingernail she indicated the message: *"Departure delayed. Plane unable to take off due to storm. Arriving Monday P.M. All our love. Mother and Dad."*

"Does that mean we have to hold up on going after Thomas Johnson?" Pete said to Donna. "I mean, with your father not here to take care of the legal end of it?"

"I don't think we should wait," Donna said. Abbey was pouring greenish tea from a pot into small Japanese cups. "Thomas Johnson may be getting the wind up — especially with his helper in a hospital someplace in Vermont, maybe spilling everything he knows."

Abbey uncovered a dish to reveal small brown wrinkled balls of something floating in a sickly yellow sauce. "Have some," she urged Pete, who dubiously spooned a small portion into a bowl filled with hot rice.

"Are we allowed to ask what this is?" Donna said as Abbey deposited a generous serving of the strange looking concoction into Donna's bowl.

"Certainly." Abbey's voice dripped Oriental courtesy. "These are Japanese fish-balls, made with lobster and shrimp, in a special sauce created for the Emperor of Japan's wedding dinner in 1654. Taste it."

Pete dipped cautiously into the bowl with his chopsticks. Everyone waited while he slowly brought it to his mouth and as slowly tasted it. His eyes closed a moment, and then he opened them wide. "Sensational!" he said with pleased surprise.

Donna said, "Abbey, this is absolutely

the best thing I ever ate! What a great idea!"

Abbey, overcome by the praise, swept her long sleeve over the table graciously. "Please. Please, have all you like." As her arm returned to her side, her sleeve swept the yellow sauce out of the serving dish and across Donna's dark blue Italian sweater. Donna stifled laughter . . . this was not the time to ruin Abbey's triumph.

"I'm going to call John Harbaugh and set things in motion first thing Monday morning," Donna said. "Something's telling me we'd better get to Thomas Johnson, but fast."

"I don't want you taking any more chances," Janet said.

"It's okay," Pete assured her. "I'm sticking to her side like glue from here to the end."

At 9:05 Monday morning, Donna, accompanied by Pete, Janet, and Abbey, who had refused to stay home, entered the law offices of Stephen Rockford. Inside, they had a hurried conference with John Harbaugh. When he had been told all the facts, he said, "It's hard to believe, but I think you're right, Donna. The question is, how do we nail him?"

"I think we should go right to his office and confront him with what we know," Donna said. "Why can't we do that?"

"We can," John Harbaugh said. "I think we'd better call first."

A terrible sense of urgency began to grip Donna as she watched John dial Thomas Johnson's number. And it increased when she heard him say to someone at the other end, "Oh, he's not in? When do you expect him? . . . Oh, he did? Not today. I see." He hung up, disappointed.

"He phoned his office to say he won't be in today," he explained.

Donna said, "We've got to see him — even if we have to go to his house. We can't wait."

"You sure?" John said.

"I'm sure," Donna answered. "Do you have his address? You said my father used to meet him a lot."

John was consulting a small phone book. "I've got it. It's in Hampstead, quite a distance out of Philadelphia."

"Let's go," Pete said.

"Wait," Donna said. She turned to John. "Can you check out a will quickly if I give you the name and approximate date?"

"Yes. I have a friend in the Surrogate

252

Division. We've been known to do favors for each other."

"Great," Donna said. "Check it out and meet us at Hampstead."

"Okay — you're the boss," John Harbaugh said.

Thomas Wingdale Johnson's home was a showplace. A huge Tudor house — a small castle, really — was centered in a heavily wooded estate of twenty-five acres located in the fashionable suburb. Pete's Pinto looked ludicrously out of place as he pulled it to a halt at the imposing entrance.

At the front door, Pete rapped the heavy bronze knocker against the door several times before a huge hatchet-faced houseman in black uniform opened the door.

"What is it?" he asked sullenly.

"Is Mr. Johnson in?" Donna asked.

"What do you want to see him for?"

Donna took the plunge. "I'm Jane Cross, from the U. of P. *Tattler*. I wrote this article about Mr. Johnson and he said he wanted to see it before we print it."

The man motioned them indoors. "Stay here," he said. "I'll find out."

He strode off down the long dark corridor and disappeared off to the left. The three stood waiting, but Donna was the one who spoke first.

"Look!" she whispered, indicating the paintings and statuary that lined the corridor. "They're old masters. They're worth a fortune."

"I wonder where Thomas Johnson got the money to buy all this out of his law practice," Pete said.

"I don't," Donna said meaningfully.

Abbey said, raising her eyebrows and indicating the collected art treasures with a broad sweep of her arm, "Ral-ley, I could be quite at home here. Don't you think it suits me, Pe-tah?"

"Abbey! Won't you ever stop?" Donna said, but then broke off as the huge man reappeared at the end of the corridor.

As the man approached, he began, "Mister Johnson says just leave the stuff and he'll read it later . . ."

Pete looked at Donna questioningly. She shook her head. "I think we have to," Donna said almost regretfully.

Pete nodded curtly and he said to the man, "You heard what the lady said. We want to see Mr. Johnson — in person."

The man's face became ugly. He stepped close to Pete and said, "I told you to leave it. So leave it and get out of here! Now!" Then, as Pete did not move, "I mean it, Buster."

"So do we," Pete said, dodging to the

254

left of the burly houseman. In that instant, Donna seized one of the man's wrists and raised it behind his back, as Pete grabbed the other and did the same. Then, marching the man between them as he growled with pain, Pete led the way to the clothes closet at the entrance door. In one motion, Pete shoved the man into the closet and then plastered himself against the door. "Quick," he said, "get a chair!"

"Not necessary, Pete," Donna said. "Look, there's a key right in the lock."

"Good girl," Pete said, bracing himself against the door as the man inside started pushing against it. In a moment, Donna had turned the key and the man was locked in.

"Now that we've gone this far," Pete said, "there's no turning back. I sure hope your ESP isn't skunking us up."

"So do I," Donna said as they quietly but swiftly made their way down the passageway. "So do I."

By this time, they were outside a huge pair of oak doors that led off to the left at the end of the passage. For a moment, they listened outside, ears to the door.

Then Donna said, "He's not alone. You heard?"

"Yeah, there's someone with him," Pete said.

255

Donna turned to Abbey. "Please," she said. "I'd feel so much better if you waited out here."

"And miss all the fun?" Abbey said. Then she added, dramatically, "Whatever happens, I'm in this with you and Peter to the end."

Donna sighed despairingly as Pete nodded and swung the door open. Before them was a huge booklined library, with shelves reaching from floor to ceiling, and heavy red draperies covering the wall facing them. Against the wall, rising from a chair behind a mammoth desk, was Thomas Wingdale Johnson. His face was flushed and his eyes were steel pinpoints as Donna and Pete drew near, with Abbey following behind.

"What's the meaning of this?" he demanded. "I gave definite orders you were to leave your article with my houseman. Why have you chosen to disobey, Miss Cross?"

He glared at Donna, but she was not paying attention. Stopped dead in her tracks, she was staring at a familiar figure seated in a second chair beside the desk. "Why, Mrs. Fitch!" she exclaimed. "Imagine seeing you here!"

Mrs. Fitch, clad in a pearl-gray suit, wearing a dignified gray velvet cloche on her dyed red hair, drew herself up like an angry hen, sending a briefcase sliding to the floor from her lap, spilling papers out. Donna hurriedly bent down and scooped up a manila folder before Mrs. Fitch could retrieve it. A quick glance told Donna what it was.

" 'In the Matter of the Adoption of Janet Willins,' " she read. She looked quizzically at Thomas Johnson.

"Now, see here, Miss Cross . . ." he began.

"Not Cross," Donna said. "Ask *her*," indicating Mrs. Fitch, who had now risen angrily, her outraged face matching the cascade of red damask hangings behind her.

"The insolence!" Mrs. Fitch said. "I knew what sort you were the first moment you came to The Perry Home, Miss Rockford."

"Did you?" Donna said. "Is that why you refused to give Janet and me the information we asked for . . . that she was entitled to?"

Mr. Johnson said impatiently, "Look, Miss Cross — or whatever your name is — I'm a busy man. I demand you leave at once. If you want to see me, you can phone my secretary and make an appointment for tomorrow at my office."

Donna said coolly, "I don't think you'll

be here tomorrow, Mr. Johnson. You're planning to take a trip, aren't you?"

Mr. Johnson blinked his eyes, then moved to his desk and sat down. "What makes you think that?" he asked.

"Just a hunch," Donna said cheerily. "You see, when it becomes common knowledge that Janet Bryson, alias Janet Willins" — she waved the manila folder before him — "when people learn how you cheated Janet Willins, Donald Johnson's child, out of the fortune that was left to her, I don't think you'll be very popular in Philadelphia, do you?"

Mr. Johnson pulled the top drawer of his desk open and removed a small, shiny, black metallic object from it. A .45 calibre Smith & Wesson snub-nosed revolver, barely the size of a child's water pistol. He raised it and leveled it directly at Donna, who was standing in front of his desk.

Beside him, Mrs. Fitch opened astonished blue eyes and said, "Why, Mr. Johnson! What in the world are you doing?"

"Shut up, you idiot!" he hissed at her, never taking his eyes off Donna. "If it weren't for your stupid babbling, I'd have been out of here long before they got here! All I wanted was the folder with the records. But you had to sit here, like a fool . . ."

"Ohh!" Mrs. Fitch sank into her chair, a wild look of disbelief in her eyes.

Mr. Johnson turned his attention to Pete. "You seem like a reasonable young man. If you are, you know that I mean it when I say that I want you to remain in this room with these three women . . ." He spat the word "women" out with contempt. He reached behind him and ripped the telephone from the wall. "There are no windows in this room, as you can see. And with no phone, you can't possibly stop me." He paused for breath, then said directly to Donna: "So you're Janet Bryson's friend. Just wouldn't give up, would you? A snip like you, a schoolgirl, a nobody. You got an idea in your head and you couldn't let go." He shook his head. "After all the good I've done."

"And the bad you've done," Donna said softly.

"Shut up! Not another word out of you!" His face was livid. He raised his gun and swept it across the figures of Pete, Donna, and Mrs. Fitch, who stood unmoving, watching him.

"I'm leaving here, and no one is stopping me. If anyone tries, I'll shoot to kill." He said to Pete, in man-to-man fashion, "You know that I will, don't you? I have nothing to lose."

"Oh, no!" It was a high, shrill cry off to his right from Abbey, her death-white face highlighted by the lush crimson of the silk hanging behind her. "No! I cahn't bear it another moment," and as Mr. Johnson turned toward her, she raised one delicate arm, clutched the draperies with a beringed hand, and with brown-tinted nails seizing them in a death grip, swooned gracefully to the ground. The damask hangings, jolted from their moorings, dropped to the floor, encompassing her fallen figure and — Mr. Johnson.

In a flash, Donna and Pete were beside him. Pete flung himself on the body of Mr. Johnson, clearly outlined underneath the hangings, while Donna helped a disarrayed Abbey out from under.

"Are you all right?" Donna asked anxiously.

"Quite," Abbey said, smoothing her hair, then anxiously looking at her left hand. "Darn, I broke my longest nail!"

"Call the police," Pete said. He had retrieved Mr. Johnson's gun and was now seated atop the back of the Philadelphia State Senator, who looked as if the end of the world had come. Which indeed it had — for him.

Chapter 19

By the time the police came, there was no further resistance left in Thomas Johnson. It was hard for the officers of the law to believe that this man — a respected State Senator — had indeed threatened their lives by armed force.

"Let me explain," John Harbaugh said to the police. He had arrived with Janet only moments before the police came.

"It's all spelled out in here," John said, flourishing a long legal paper with blue backing. " 'The Last Will and Testament of Donald Johnson.' I don't know the amount, but it appears to be well in excess of five million dollars."

"But that's a civil suit," the officer began.

"Not when the one who stole the money is trying to leave the country," Donna said. "Look, over there." She walked to where a pair of suitcases stood. "I saw them sticking out from beneath the draper-

ies before my sister yanked them down."
Then she crossed over to where Thomas
Johnson stood between two policemen. She
began to reach for his jacket, but before
she could, one of the policemen put his hand
inside to an inner pocket and extracted a
green envelope with the words "World
Airlines" printed across the face of it.

The patrolman whistled softly. "Whew!
Looks like you're right about that," he said.
"You a detective or something?"

"Not yet," Donna said.

"You'd make a darn good one, sister,"
the policeman said grudgingly.

"Thanks ... brother," Donna said, grinning.

When the police had left with Mr. Johnson in custody, a strangely softened Mrs.
Fitch tried to explain. "Really, really I
had no idea," she stopped. Then she began
again. This time she addressed herself directly to Janet. "Mr. Johnson seemed un-
usually interested in your case, Miss ..."
She laughed a nervous little titter. "But
he's such a famous man, I had no idea,
none at all ..." She stopped, abashed.

"It's all right," Janet said. "I understand, I think."

"No, Janet. Don't make it so easy for
her," Donna said. "There's a whole home-

ful of babies, children, in the same boat that you were in." She turned to Mrs. Fitch. "Who's got the money, or the famous name, or even . . . a legitimate name — that's not what matters, Mrs. Fitch. You have to take each person separately. Once you start to look at their labels, you get in trouble."

Then, as Mrs. Fitch still said nothing, Donna added, "I'd try to do a better job after this if I were you, Mrs. Fitch. Because people will be watching to see how things are in The Perry Home."

Five of them were gathered around a big table in Pagano's. In the center of it were a Super Special Pizza, a Mindblowing Meatball Submarine three-foot-long hero sandwich, and all the trimmings.

John Harbaugh beamed at Janet. "You, Janet Bryson, are Donald Johnson's sole heir."

Janet blushed. "I can't believe it. Why me?"

"Hush, Jan. If you're going to be a millionaire — and I'm afraid you are — you're going to have to act like one," Donna said.

"I don't know how," Janet said. "What do I do?"

"I wouldn't know," Donna said. "The most money I've ever had in my life is $400.00 my parents gave me one Christmas, and I spent it all on a fabulous fake fur coat and furnishing my share of our apartment, Jan."

"Yeah." Janet's eyes were serious. "Why *fake* fur?"

"You're getting off the subject," John Harbaugh said. "Janet can now buy anything she wants. That's what motivated Thomas Johnson . . . all that money."

"I'm not sure I understand," Pete said.

"When Donald Johnson I made his will, he clearly stated that when he died, his fortune was to go to his wife; if she did not survive him, the money would go to his son, Donald Johnson II. If Donald Johnson II did not survive, it would go to his *issue* — that means children — if any. If there was no issue, the entire fortune would be left to his nephew, Thomas Johnson."

"I get it," Donna said. "Donald Johnson must have written to his cousin Thomas telling him about the baby . . ."

"Right again," John Harbaugh said. "That's just what happened. And since Thomas Johnson was the attorney for Donald Johnson I, Thomas knew what the will said."

Donna's eyes lit with comprehension. "Then that explains it."

"Explains what?" Janet said, her brows furrowed.

"All those attempts on your life," Donna explained. "Probably beginning with the break-in of our apartment."

"I have a statement here," John Harbaugh said, consulting a sheaf of notepaper before him. He looked from Donna to Janet as he explained. "The man you saw at the funeral was Thomas Johnson himself. From the moment he got that letter from his cousin notifying him that a girl named Ellen Willins was having a child — his child — Thomas Johnson knew he would never inherit his uncle's vast fortune. But when his uncle's entire family was wiped out in the plane crash, he saw his opportunity. He kept careful vigilance on Ellen Willins, and even became a trustee of The Perry Home to which she finally had to give her baby."

"That way he could keep track of the baby — of Janet — even when she was given out for adoption," Donna said, excited.

"Smart girl," John Harbaugh said. "That's why he did it. After Mr. Bryson's funeral, Thomas Johnson went out to Janet's house and hung around long enough the night you two girls were alone to hear that Janet intended to find out who her *real* parents were."

"That must have driven him wild," Donna said. "If Janet was really determined to find out who her mother and father were, Thomas Johnson knew that one day he'd have to give up the fortune he inherited nineteen years before, when Janet's father was killed."

"Exactly," John Harbaugh said. "But he's not a young man, and the job of stopping Janet was too much for him to handle alone. So he hired a gangster — "

Donna broke in again. "A hit man! Someone who contracts to get rid of a person someone wants out of the way. The man I saw in his office."

"Right," John said. "At first he thought he'd just have his gangster chum scare you off. That's why your apartment got messed up, and your pictures ripped off the class photo. But it didn't work." John smiled at Donna. "You don't scare easily."

"So as Janet and I got closer and closer to the truth," Donna said, "he must have gotten more and more desperate."

"Check," John said, looking over his notes. "His statement says, 'The assault on Janet Bryson on the university grounds was intended to injure, not kill, her. The assault by automobile in the parking lot, however, was to maim her permanently or kill her, if need be.'" John said grimly, "Friendly fellow, isn't he?"

Janet shuddered. "How about the attack on Donna in Florida?"

"According to these notes, his orders to the mobster were to see that you were not to leave Florida alive, Janet," John said. "Since you and Donna are generally the same size and coloring, Donna became the intended victim by sheer accident."

"And the same thing happened up on the slope in Vermont?" Donna said speculatively. John nodded.

Donna said, "We looked so much alike in our ski clothes, he was fooled again. And — that explains why they found no identification on his clothing. He's probably a criminal known to the police."

John Harbaugh raised a forkful of pasta to his mouth. "I salute you, Donna. You've got it all figured out." He turned to Janet. "Do you have any idea how rich you are, young lady?" He brought forth an envelope on which some figures were hastily scribbled in pencil. "Thomas Johnson had $1,200 in 1957. In 1958, when the will was settled, he inherited five million dollars in cash. He is currently worth twice that. Unless I don't know my law, you'll be entitled to most of it."

Pete turned to Janet. "Will you marry me? I've suddenly fallen in love." He grinned at Donna.

Janet laughed, "You're kidding, Pete. But I wonder if everybody else will be. Would you believe? When I called Dennis in Florida this afternoon to tell him, his mother insisted on talking to me. She said she always knew I came from a 'good family,' and that was why she felt it was important for me to find out." She spread her hands wide with palms upward and said to Donna, "Do you believe it? Mrs. Macfarland?"

"That's the price of having Dennis for a husband," Donna said. "Every now and then you'll have to deal with his mother — your mother-in-law."

"Dennis is worth it," Janet said.

"How did you like my performance?" Abbey asked. "Wasn't my fainting act in the library glorious?"

Donna bent over and kissed her sister on the cheek. "Abbey, you're a kook, and the way you act, half the time I don't know if you're Scarlett O'Hara or the Queen of Egypt. But you're terrific!"

Abbey leaned over toward Pete and said, "Did you hear that, Pe-tah?"

"Except when you act like that," Donna said. "When will you believe that vamps went out with Gloria Swanson in 1928?"

Pete said, across the table, "So now, I suppose I have to start accepting the fact that the love of my life is going to be a detective, a female Charlie Chan. Is that so?" He waited for Donna's answer.

"Confucius say, Pete Kelly right, as usual," Donna said.

"Well, if you've really decided, what I can't understand is why you look so worried," Pete said.

"What I'm thinking about is how I'm going to tell Mother and Dad when they get back tonight," Donna said.

"Don't worry. Leave it to me," Abbey said. "By the time I explain — in my own special way — they'll be begging you to open your own private investigation agency."

Donna reached across the table and seized her sister's hand. "If anyone can do it, you can."

Pete said to Abbey, "Listen, since you're so terrific at that kind of thing, do you think you can talk your sister into becoming Mrs. Pete Kelly some day?"

"Ms.," Donna said. "It would be Ms. *Donna* Kelly, even Ms. Donna Rockford-Kelly."

Pete's eyes lit up. "You mean — you will marry me some day?"

Donna said, "Well, we'll see, Pete. Time will tell."

Abbey fluttered her long lashes at Pete. "Don't worry, Pe-tah, don't worry," she said. "Just leave everything to Abbey."